THE DE... THE AUGUST BODY W... INTERRUPTED BY A RAP AT THE DOOR

Undersecretary Crodfoller turned to rebuke the intruder, but the reprimand died on his lips as he was greeted by the entrance of a tall, broad-shouldered man clad in a scorched and torn garment barely recognizable as a CDT issue coverall.

"What's this, sir?" Crodfoller barked. "Your appearance is disgraceful!"

"Not nearly as disgraceful as his *dis*appearance, Mr. Undersecretary," Magnan objected, jumping up excitedly. "Retief," he went on more calmly, addressing the newcomer, "we'd heard you'd been captured by the insidious Ree, out on Icebox Nine!"

"Not quite, Mr. Magnan," Retief replied coolly. "I spotted them landing, and decided to surround them, just in case."

"Surround them?" Crodfoller echoed hollowly. "You did nothing to create an impression of hostility, I hope!"

Retief soothed the great man. "Captain Fump didn't complain. He got interested in my gun collection, and hardly uttered a word."

WITH BONUS RETIEF NOVELETTE!

KEITH LAUMER

THE RETURN OF RETIEF

A BAEN BOOK

THE RETURN OF RETIEF

This is a work of fiction. All the characters and events portrayed in this book are fictional, and any resemblance to real people or incidents is purely coincidental.

A Baen Books Original

Baen Enterprises
260 Fifth Avenue
New York, N.Y. 10001

First printing, September 1984
Second printing, December 1985

ISBN: 0-671-55902-8

Cover art by Wayne Barlowe

Printed in the United States of America

Distributed by
SIMON & SCHUSTER
MASS MERCHANDISE SALES COMPANY
1230 Avenue of the Americas
New York, N.Y. 10020

CAST OF CHARACTERS

Members of the *Corps Diplomatique Terrestrienne*

Retief—Envoy-At-Large (that is, at large if he's lucky)

Ben Magnan—Economic Officer (and apple-polisher *par excellence*)

Hy Felix—Information Service Attaché (especially attached to his prospective retirement pension)

Ambassador Morris Sidesaddle (a bungler with pigeon-bellied suavity)

Temporary Acting Deputy Undersecretary Hercules Crodfoller (great note-taker of his colleagues' faults)

Deputy Undersecretary "Tubby" Shortfall

Career Minister Homer Sitzfleisch (advocate of forceful chumship)

Undersecretary Clayfoot (skeptical Staff Duty Officer, Sector HQ)

First Secretary and Cultural Attaché Chester Underthrust (an old hand, career-wise)

General Services Officer Marvin Lackluster (a tyro learning the ropes)

Political Officer Henry Hencrate

Assistant Political Officer Elmer Proudfoot

Colonel Stanley Trenchfoot, Military Attaché

General Ralph Otherday

In addition: Eustace, Clarence, Jerry the barman, and a cast of pen-pushers, obstructors, and obfuscators

The Ree
(tentacles at one end and frills at the other)
Captain Fump (a moron, not especially happy)
Goop (Fump's crewman, none too bright)
Captain Biff (trader of glimp eggs)
Intimidator Slive (six-foot-six column of deceit and other diplomatic ploys)

The Groaci
(five-eyed, crested, with weak throat sacs)
Consul Snith (a go-between, playing both sides of the street)
In addition: belligerent Groaci Legation Guards and a sweet female secretary

The Prutians
(single-visioned, several-armed)
Chief Health Inspector Thise
Civilian Chief Gluck
Jake, the ubiquitous cab driver
In addition: LeRoy, Horace, the Yill Captain M'hu hu, assorted cops

Pushy, the Goblin(s) of Goblinrock
(telepathic, yellow—when not being purple or pink—mobile cactus—except when being blue tendrils or puffballs)

The Terran Pioneers
Sergeant-Major Grundy (Home Guard boss on Hardtack)
Governor Anderson & Family (Ree hostages)
Chief Heavy Charlie Two-Spears (No. 1 Big Medicine)

Princess Sally (Matriarch from Jawbone)

Powerful Pete (King *pro tem* from Drygulch)

Cap Josh (ex-pug from Shivaree)

Chief Umbulu (Moosejaw brass)

Boss Nandy (tough, but not tough enough)

Tang the Execrable (robber baron from Drywash)

Stan Spewak (who knew which side of the Arm had the armaments)

Prologue

The landscape was one of endless ice under a vast, black sky. Great towering blue-green cliffs alternated with tumbled fields of immense, ragged-edged pristine white slabs heaved up and shattered by the inexorable advance of the glacial masses sliding relentlessly down from the naked heights exposed here and there as remorseless gravity stripped them of their compacted snow mantles. Harsh winds swept dust-sized ice-particles up into swirling clouds and abrasive streamers which scoured the exposed ice and deposited graceful drifts in the lee of every obstruction, a fluffy, floury layer which concealed crevasses and obscured the underlying ice forms.

The faint, yellowish light of the minor main sequence star known as Icebox shed a wan, late-afternoon glow over the scene, casting deep blue shadows and striking golden highlights from ridges and peaks, evoking dull glints from flat surfaces, making the ice-clouds glow as if from fires raging within them, a brilliant display against the black sky, wherein less than a dozen stars were visible, though the Arm was a dusty glow arching from horizon to horizon; and near it, three of the eight inner worlds of the Icebox system hung like polished marbles, being, like Icebox, ice-worlds with high albedos.

In the inadequate shelter of a long, meandering strike fault in the county-wide slab which had once been a minor sea until frozen solid and at last heaved from its basin by the encroaching glacier, there could be seen the single intrusive element in the otherwise pristine wilderness; a one-man environment-bubble, anchored in place by cables attached to bedrock deep below the ice-surface, and already, after only seventy-two hours, sunk a foot deep in the ice. Inside the polarized dome sat a tall, broad-shouldered man wearing the pale-blue-and-gold class three coverall prescribed by the *Corps Diplomatique Terrestrienne* for diplomatic personnel serving on pre-nuclear worlds, informal occasions, for wear on. His name was Retief, CDTO-5, Second Secretary and Consul, detached duty. He sat before a field-model surveillance screen, watching the unsteady approach of a small craft which the IFF circuitry had identified as an assault boat of the Ree Expeditionary Force, hesitantly inbound on a contact course. So the reports pouring in from outpost worlds here in Tip Space were at least partly true: the Arm was being probed, as the Deep-Think teams back at Sector had determined, by an explosively breeding race known as the Ree, perhaps from the Western Arm.

The alien craft approached swiftly, dropped from view half a mile distant into a hollow among the towering ice-peaks, an impact crater from an ancient meteorite, which Retief had explored on his first day at the isolated outpost. The small plain at its center was suitably level, well sheltered from surprise attack, unlike the bubble exposed on the ice-plain. Retief switched on the recorder and proceeded with his hourly formal report:

"Monitor station twenty-three, Icebox Nine, hour seventy-two, Retief: a hundred tonner ID'd as a Ree Class Two unit made a non-sked approach, perhaps in distress, and is now on surface. So far, no overt action. Hold for copy of incoming on Ree frequency."

Retief tuned the all-bands receiver, its ACTIVE light blinking furiously, thinned out the star-static, and heard an irascible voice say in curiously-accented Terran:

"Ho, we see bubble you hid in plain sight. This trick don't work on me. You come out now."

"Hold!" Retief dictated into the recorder. "I'm picking up static on the attack band; looks like a leak-over from a build-up on an old-fashioned pulse cannon—"

A deafening blast rocked the bubble, enveloped it in a blinding flash which faded to reveal a whirling cloud of ice particles churning beyond the tough, transparent membrane. The concussion had opened a long crack across the clear dome, and warm air was rushing out, to turn at once to a jet of white ice crystals. As the roar of churning ice subsided, Retief heard the Ree voice, speaking in the same impatient tone, as if nothing had happened.

"I figgered out if I blow you up first, you can't carry out no fell designs against us. Only I found out the steering gadget on my command here don't work. This is a distress signal, and you gotta come over and give us a hand, or maybe I'll get mad and shoot you again. If you're still alive, that is. If not, disregard. Now hurry up, because I get tired holding down this HOLD button on our automatic attack gear."

Retief checked the recorder; the idiot lights indicated all systems go. . . . He resumed his report, "Did you catch that amazing sample of Ree logic? Are there any more at home like him? We now suspend this broadcast, for investigative purposes. Stay tuned, folks!"

He switched the recorder to SEND and transmitted the report in a .01 picosecond squirt to Sector, then donned the weather suit which had been fitted to him at the supply station where the bubble had been prepared. He checked to be sure the aftermarket energy gun was in place on his hip, its flow-rate indicator showing full gain. Unlike the otherwise similar detached model weapon limited to a self-contained .1 kiloton/second energy slug, this one drew on the suit's 3 k/s power pack.

Retief cycled the airlock and jumped down into the relentless buffeting of the full gale which was a Spring day on Icebox Nine. On foot, he made his way toward the pass, like a knife-cut through the rim of ice which concealed the alien vessel. His head was still ringing from the concussion so close to his shelter, which now lay canted at a steep angle in the crater formed by the near-miss, but aside from the crack apparently undamaged.

His suit's power assist system made it barely possible to walk on the slippery and uneven surface against the gusty wind, upslope. He reached the crest of the trail cut long ago by a final outflow of liquid nitrogen, paused in the deep blue shadow, and saw below the squat, stepped-on looking vessel, its polished hull bright with colored inlays against the black ice. Around it, stubby figures in day-glo suits moved apparently aimlessly, then abruptly formed up in ragged ranks, right-faced, and set off purposefully directly toward the pass. Retief watched them for a moment, then, setting the dispersion adjustment on his heat-gun at its narrowest aperture, he carefully melted a deep incision in the ice-wall beside him, studied the resultant pattern of stress-cracks and fracture planes, then climbed atop a fallen ice-block to make another deep, flat cut, which converged toward, but did not quite meet the first.

The aliens were still marching directly toward him, but showed no signs of noticing him, or the modest steam-clouds his work had produced. He laid low until the Ree column had passed, then, at the top of the pass, he paused, swung, and at tight beam burned through one of the now exposed anchor cables restraining the bubble; it turned lazily and slid down into the blast crater, entry-port down.

The Ree soldiery, having filed through the pass and deployed before the bubble, dithered in confusion, then fell into ranks again and stood unmoving, their face plates staring skyward.

Retief made his way down the rough path to

the crater floor; there he paused, turned, studied the iceberg for a moment, then took careful aim with his energy gun at narrow beam, and cut away the last bridge of ice supporting the immense mass he had earlier cut almost free. At last, a sharp *crack*! rang out, followed by a deep-noted rumble. The entire face of the towering ice sheet began to descend, shattered suddenly into myriad pieces, some no larger than dice, others as big as pianos. With a deafening roar, the ice cascaded down, closing the pass under a drift of frozen methane, wreathed in a slowly settling cloud of ice crystals.

He went on toward the alien vessel; when he was within a hundred yards of it, the amplified voice boomed out:

"We see you! Thought for a minute the ice fall got you. Now approach, more slow but hurry up!"

As the amplified command came to an end, Retief noticed that the turret-mounted gun which had been aimed toward the pass was now rotating and depressing steeply so as to bear directly on him. He advanced slowly, passed into the shelter of the alien hull, while the guns reached maximum deflection and came to rest with a whine of frustrated gearing.

At the stern of the vessel, Retief examined the adjacent ice-wall, studied angles and distances, and again made two converging cuts in the clean blue ice.

Behind him, the same irritable voice spoke up again: "I notice the pass fell in, just missed my fellows. Looks like maybe you tried to put one over on me."

"What do you mean, 'tried'?" Retief asked,

using an inductance contact unit which he held against the space-burned hull plate beside him.

"You better come out where I can see you, stranger," the alien cut, "or otherwise I can't shoot you if we feel like it. Maybe you say no fair ask for help, then shoot you when you come over. Well, that's a little trick we played on you, crafty stranger."

"Worked fine," Retief said. "And here I am. Now you'd better open up so I can come in and have a nice chat with you. Otherwise I'll have to bury your command under an estimated five hundred tons of ice. That's a little trick *I* played on *you*."

"Now you better come inside my vehicle and give me your explanation and apologies," the Ree said as if by sudden inspiration. The entry hatch cycled open.

"When the inside door opens, come up the hall to my office," the voice commanded curtly. "See, I don't want to leave my captain-chair here, cause I might get lost. Never *did* read the Owner's Manual on this thing."

Retief left the airlock and proceeded forward to the command deck. As he went he snapped open his face plate. An alien odor of smoked fish assailed his nostrils.

In the Command Center he saw what he assumed was the Ree captain, closely fitted into a gimbal-mounted container the size of a garbage can, which exposed only a face like a burnt waffle, surrounded by muscular tentacles, which twitched suddenly, and then hung limp.

"Ho, you startled me, creeping up like that," the alien voice said, unmagnified now, and sounding like a ten-year-old Boy Scout, flunking his

Eagle badge. "When I get startled," the captain went on, "I'm no good for anything for half an hour. Takes the starch out of the old tentacles. Sit down, stranger, and wait'll I feel like it."

"Would you really have shot me, if I'd let you?" Retief inquired mildly.

"Sure, yes! See, I got these here automatic defense circuits; they're set up to blast anything comes close to the hull."

"Why didn't you shut the system down?" Retief asked. "We couldn't very well talk if you'd blasted me first."

"I don't know nothing about all that fancy electric stuff," the garbage canned Ree explained. "I hardly even got to find out how to work the autochef, otherwise I and my boys woulda starved. This is my first command."

"Why did you shoot at my station?" Retief inquired. "What are you doing on this iceberg?"

"Well, I got my orders," the Ree said, in a tone which implied he expected an argument. "Anyway, I'm asking the questions. Now, who and what are you, and why?"

"I am Retief, Terry diplomat on detached duty to monitor the automatic equipment monitoring the ice flow for Cartographic Section," Retief replied. "As for why, I'll have to pass that one. It's one of those jobs they give people they're not quite ready to shoot. I still want to know what you're doing here, and why you attacked me."

"Well, I was having a little trouble with my vehicle, Retief. By the way, I'm Captain Fump, Imperial Naval Arm of Great Ree. So, like I was telling you, my vehicle here was giving me a hard time. See, I wanted to head for some place they called Lonesome George, but it seems like my vehicle here has got this pre-programmed course set in it, and I hadda shoot a hole into the control box, before it'd leave off trying to steer itself. Then I found out it wasn't so easy to steer it good by hand, and I hadda make what you call a force landing. OK?"

"OK up to that point," Retief conceded, "but why did you fire at my bubble?"

"Ah, them automatics took over again, what you call a back-up system. Nothing I could do. Lucky you ducked in close where they can't see you, Retief, or they'da blasted you sure."

"I see," Retief replied. "That being the case, it's a good thing I didn't deploy my defensive batteries, eh? What an emplacement of infinite repeaters would do to this tub is nobody's business."

"Yeah, lucky your automatics don't work no bettern' mine," Fump said complacently. His tentacles were beginning to twitch now. "OK, I'm warming up, Retief," he said. "Be in shape in a minute. Now, the way I see it, you better go lock yourself in the aft lazaret, that means back storeroom, and I'll see if I can get my command together here, and we'll take a little ride. Now it's time for my nap." The burnt waffle went slack, and a buzzing sound started up.

He made a leisurely tour of the Groaci manufactured vessel, found a dormitory consisting of stacked garbage cans, smaller than Fump's, all empty. . . . A lone crewman, apparently the only crewman left aboard after Fump had sent the squad outside, was manning the aft fire-control compartment. The chamber was clearly in need of maintenance. Retief stripped away spider-webs and entered the cramped space.

"Hey!" the Ree gunnery officer exclaimed as Retief appeared abruptly before him. "You're a Groaci, ain't you? *Love* them Groaci; good pals, if only they wouldn't steal so much, no offense."

"You may talk about the sticky fingers of the Groaci all you like," Retief reassured the fellow. "Personally, I'm more of a Terry."

"Oh. I heard about them: got big antlers, hey, and green spots, and all, right? Sure, I seen plenty Terries even if they do eat Groaci grubs and got a terrible prejudice against all life-forms fortunate enough to have five eyes, like the Groaci. That's how come the Terries are always picking on the peace-loving Groaci, which they only wanta live peaceful."

"On someone else's real estate," Retief pointed out. "Which brings us to you boys: what are you doing so far out of your own backyard?"

"Well, we got this big invasion planned, only don't tell anybody because it's what you call Top Secret dope."

"Oh? Are there many of you Top Secret dopes?" Retief inquired.

"Sure, a big armada of us, but old Fumpy got lost—and here we are. But where in the Cold Place are we, anyway?"

"You're on a minor planet known as Icebox Nine, in the North Tip of the Eastern Arm. I take it you boys are from the Western Arm."

"Right, and if you ask me, which nobody will, we should of stayed home and reworked the tailings. I took a look outside, and I didn't see nothing but ice. Course a nice cool climate is swell, with just the odd glacier creeping down the mountain for excitement, but *this* place is ridiculous."

"So you don't intend to lay claim to Icebox Nine?" Retief inquired casually.

"Not unless old Fumpy is even dumber'n what I think he is. You know the rule: everybody stakes out a new breeding surface gets to live there, permanent, as King, or Mayor, or Emperor, or Dictator, or Count, whatever title he likes. Now, on a planet like this, what fun could a fellow have dictating, or counting, or whatever? We oughta head for home pronto, and report the invasion didn't work out. But old Fumpy's got a idear he can be a big shot, except he forgot to find out how to run this tub, which he took delivery personal from some local turncoat name of Lith, or Whish, or like that."

"You shouldn't leave your intercom open if you're gonna knock your captain," Fump's voice spoke grumpily from the wall-mounted talker. "By the way, Goop, if you see a creature with only four limbs snooping around in your department, throw a quick Kablitski on him and leave him lay in the aft lazaret. I trusted the bum to lock himself up, but he outsmarted me. Got it?"

"Eye, eye, sir," Goop replied snappily. "Hey, hold still a minute, pal," he added, addressing Retief. "I got to look up 'Kablitski' in my martial arts manual, where I can throw one on you like the cap'n said."

"Never mind," Retief suggested. "I'll just go forward and explain to the captain why that would be a bad idea."

"Well," Goop said, laying aside his manual

"Sure. If you promise you won't pull a fast one and not report to Cap like you said."

"I promise," Retief assured the yeoman.

Back in the cramped command center, Retief found Fump out of his seat and poring over a chart-table. The alien was of simple physique, being a foot-thick, four-foot-tall column of bluish-white muscle with a ring of small tentacles just below the horny face, and a rippling fringe at the lower end, by which he ambulated with surprising agility. Now he stood as if shocked when Retief confronted him.

"It's you again!" the captain charged.

"Right," Retief replied in a congratulatory tone. "I see you're too sharp to fool about that, Captain."

"Ho," Fump agreed. "What you doing back here in my office, after you said you was going back to the lock-up?"

"You missed that one," Retief said. "I didn't say I was planning on locking myself up: that was *your* idea."

"Yeah, but you lemme think—" the stubby officer started, then abruptly doubled over and spun, its upper quarters whipping toward Retief in a blow that would have broken ribs. Retief braced himself against a wall-locker and raised a knee, placed to intercept Fump's rugged face, which it did, with a meaty *smack*! The captain tottered, straightened, with thin yellow juice dribbling from his features, and staggered back.

"Hoo, that really smarted!" he wailed. "I done that zinger just like it says in the handbook, and it didn't work! No fair! Course, you ain't built like a Ree—if you would've been a Ree that woulda smacked you right square in the nerve plexus." He fingered a pinkish patch on his pale, muscular torso. "Woulda took the starch outa you," he added. Fump paused to massage his face gently, wiping the exudate on his desk blotter.

"Never mind," Retief said comfortingly. "After all, it's not as if you planned to try it again."

"*Another* zinger?" Fump echoed in a shocked tone. "The handbook says *one* will do it every time. See, us Ree got this reasonable sorta approach: if it looks like we're losing, we lay off and estivate until the coast is clear. If we're winning, of course we take charge. Like now: I figgered with you alone and on foot, and me here with my vehicle, which has got plenty firepower, *I* was in charge; anybody'd of done the same. But now, while I got this here furb-ache, it seems like maybe I shoulda played it a little different." Fump's tentacles caressed his furb gently.

"That's all right," Retief reassured the captain. "No harm done. The strategy now is to make friends, right?"

"What for?" Fump asked wonderingly. "That ain't in the handbook."

"Never mind," Retief told Fump. "The first friendly item is for you to relinquish this vehicle without the need for me to do anything violent; that wouldn't be friendly, you know."

"Figgers," Fump acknowledged. "Well, it's the breaks of the game, I guess. What you want with my vehicle, anyway?"

"Thought I might use it to go home in," Retief explained. "Since you carelessly cracked my bubble, I've got no place to stay."

"What am I s'pose to tell Sneak Command?" the captain demanded.

"Just tell them the truth," Retief suggested. "That you lent it to a friend."

"And what if I don't?" Fump demanded. "Hand it over, I mean," he amplified.

"Why worry about that?" Retief queried. "Since it isn't going to happen."

"Sure, no use borrowing trouble," the Ree agreed. "See how friendly I can be?" He was edging toward a wall locker, Retief noted.

"You don't want anything from the arms locker, do you, Captain?" Retief asked casually.

Fump halted abruptly. "Funny you should ask that," he said. "I was just going to show you where I keep my hand-guns."

"Later," Retief said, and spun the combination dial on the locker, causing the tumblers inside the vault-like door to seat with a complicated *click!* Behind him, Fump spoke into his PA talker:

"Assault squad, to the bridge on the double."

"They won't be coming," Retief told Fump. "They seem to be trapped on the far side of the pass."

"I saw it fall in," Fump acknowledged. "But I was hoping maybe they hadn't got that far yet."

"It's all right," Retief said soothingly. "I can handle this thing well enough, single-handed. But I wouldn't want you to be tempted to get into mischief behind my back, while I'm busy at the controls. So maybe I'd better just shoot you."

"Who, me?" Fump wailed. "You wouldn't do that, Retief, after we been pals and all!"

"There might be an alternative," Retief mused. "Do you happen to have an old potato bag aboard? Or a grenade sack, anything big enough for you to fit in it."

"*Me* fit in it?" Fump asked. "What for?"

"Because if you object, you might get another furb-ache," Retief explained patiently. "After which the question of shooting you would arise again."

"Durn," Fump said. "What good is a command with commandees that're someplace else?"

"You don't seem to feel much sympathy for your boys," Retief observed. "They must be frozen solid by now."

"Sure, but freezing don't hurt us Rees. We evolved from bottom-feeders, you know, hadda get through the winter when the ponds froze solid, so no sweat. I can send a warm-up squad in for them in a few years and thaw 'em out and they'll be as happy as clams."

"That's handy for extended campaigns in cold country," Retief commented. "But it also makes them rather vulnerable to being dozed up and captured."

"No fair telling," Fump reminded his captor. "It's a kind of what you call a military secret and all."

"I wouldn't dream of betraying military secrets," Retief said. He stepped around Fump and tapped the intercom button. "Ho there, Goop," he said. "Your captain wants you to bring a large sack."

"What for?"

"Yours not to reason why. Just bring it."

"Eye, eye, I guess."

A few moments later the gunnery officer appeared, carrying a folded sack of tough, greenish polyon, clearly of Groaci manufacture.

Retief took the sack. "Thank you, Goop," he said politely. "You may go back to your sweeping and dusting."

Goop ruffled a tentacle. "What's that?"

"Study the Crew Manual. About face! March!" Goop, looking dazed, withdrew.

Fump eyed the capacious bag and sighed. "You ain't never gonna get me in that," he said with finality.

"How's your furb-ache feeling?" Retief asked kindly.

"It's holding up good," Fump replied. "You don't need to freshen it up none."

"That won't be necessary," Retief reassured the discouraged fellow. "Now, I could just order you outside, or shoot you here, if you prefer."

"Probably go off and leave me here to freeze up solid," Fump predicted. "That ain't fatal, but it smarts some; I shoulda filled up on Prestone like the troops. SOP for surface ops on these here ice-hells," he explained.

"It's just as well," Retief said. "You won't need it."

"You mean—you're really gonna kill me—in cold blood?" Fump inquired in a faltering tone. "Looky, fella, I never figgered on this, as I'd of never let you inside my vehicle."

"I don't intend to plug unless I see you outside that bag four seconds from now," Retief reassured the Ree. "OK?"

"That's not hardly OK," Fump came back. "But I got no choice, I guess. You gonna keep me inside this here poke now?"

"Soon, Cap," Retief informed his captive. "It's a lot of work, but it's the only alternative to shooting you, and I need you alive, up to a point."

"Oh," Fump replied glumly. "I was kind of hoping you'd accept my parole or something, and leave me have a chance to use my firepower. But you outsmarted me. OK, let's get to it." He submitted meekly as Retief pulled the sack over him and secured the top.

"They can't say I abandoned my command," Fump boasted muffledly. "Even if I *am* kinda cramped up in this here specimen sack. How's about you let me out now, and I'll put in a good word for you when the relief expedition arrives. The one I'm gonna send out a call for as soon as I get a chance, I mean."

"Actually, Captain," Retief replied. "I think for the present you'd best remain where you are; later I'll put you in the aft lazaret. But no distress signals. Anyway, we won't be here long."

"Whattya mean we won't be here long?"

"I have to be back at Sector for some sort of a tribal pow-wow," Retief told the Ree. "So just get busy estivating, and I'll see how good your lift gear is."

"You don't mean yer gonna try and lift my vehicle without my say-so?" Fump demanded indignantly.

"I thought I might," Retief conceded.

"Don't try it, Terry," Fump warned. "You activate all that machinery wrong and she'll blow sky-high."

"Don't worry," Retief soothed the excited Ree. "I'll read the Owner's Manual."

Chapter One

Sector Headquarters of the *Corps Diploma-tique Terrestrienne* at Aldo Cerise was a hundred-story slab of glass and blackish-gold eka-bronze, rising from a velvet-green lawn ornamented with the picturesque ruins of an angel fountain which had adorned a formal garden built on the site twenty-three thousand years before. The remainder of the ancient tiled street was essentially intact, lined with the vari-colored ceramic-faced palaces of the long-dead aristocrats of the deserted world.

A group of five Terrans disembarked from the CDT spinner which had transported them from the port which lay well beyond the limits of this long-dead city, on a deserted world of an alien star.

"This place always gives me the, ah, 'creeps' is the appropriate term, I believe," said Ben Magnan, currently serving as First Economic Secretary. His thin, narrow shoulders shuddered

as his gaze darted along the silent avenue which
thirty thousand years (standard) before had
echoed to the tread of victorious legions.

"Cripes, Ben," muttered Hy Felix, the Information Service Attache. "Can't you just say the
joint gives you the creeps just like it does
everybody, without making it sound like a bail-
out clause in a treaty?"

"This, gentlemen," Career Ambassador Sidesaddle rebuked sternly, "is not the time for
creeps, faced as we are with an awkward negotiation with a *de facto* invader of Terrestrial space."

"What's so awkward about it, Mr. Ambassador?" inquired Colonel Trenchfoot, the newly-
assigned Military Attaché, with only a touch of
his well-known irascibility. "All we have to do
is tell 'em to scram, right?"

The Ambassador turned on the colonel a look
of Restrained Impatience (621-C), not unmixed
with Greatness Sorely Tried (623-N). "That, my
dear Colonel," he said coolly, "is hardly the
diplomatic spirit, if I may say so. Perhaps you've
not yet had time to read through the orientation
binder, providing as it does the background to
the present conference to which we've been
summoned." The great man glanced at his watch,
then up at the classical stainless steel facade
which graced the ground-level entry, where two
Marines in dress blues stood at parade rest.

"Sure, Chief, I read all that jazz," the colonel
replied testily. "I still say if we run a bluff on
them they'll fold like a three-card flush to a
hundred-C raise."

"The allusion, one assumes," Sidesaddle returned coldly, "is to some ruffianly game of
chance, which is precisely the diametrical oppo-

site of the scientifically exact approach of enlightened diplomacy, which alone proffers hope of an equitable accommodation with the insidious Ree."

"Give these suckers an inch and they'll take a couple of lights," the colonel said stubbornly garbled (37-M).

"Your 37 requires work, Trenchfoot," His Excellency rebuked mildly. "I suggest you supplement your other professional reading with a re-perusal of the handbook *Alien Organ Clusters and How to Read Them*, I believe it's titled."

"Unless the rot runs even deeper than the rumors have it," the military man responded doggedly, "there's no aliens in HQ for me to read their organ clusters."

"Wait'll you meet some of these headquarters types, Stan," Information Attache Felix put in. "Maybe the rumors ain't so far off after all," a remark which netted him a frigid stare from the Ambassador. Before the situation could deteriorate further, the eerie silence was broken by a distant whining as of a giant and ill-tempered hornet, followed a moment later by a *boom!* which dislodged a number of tiles from the facades along the avenue to fall and shatter on the paving below. Immediately thereafter, a grotesque atmosphere craft of clearly alien design darted into view from behind the clustered towers and braked sharply to overfly the street on a strafing run.

"Gentlemen," Ambassador Sidesaddle intoned, over the chatter of bore-guns, "it appears we are witness to a breach of diplomatic etiquette of the grossest description." His pronouncement fell on empty air, however, since his colleagues were by this time halfway to the shadowy entry; noting which, Sidesaddle himself broke into a heavy trot toward shelter.

"Gracious, Mr. Ambassador," Magnan burbled, as his chief arrived to take shelter between the two Marines, now standing at rigid attention. "That was a near thing! I *do* admire the way your Excellency stood your ground until the bullets were practically ripping up the pavement at your feet—but wasn't it just the teensiest bit foolhardy?"

"Perhaps, Magnan," His Excellency conceded modestly, "I was overbold. Still, perhaps the attack was only an expression of boyish exuberance on the part of a Ree pilot, without official sanction, and thus not an interplanetary incident worthy of response as such."

"The bullets still could have smarted," Hy Felix grunted, gazing after the receding craft as it finished its run and disappeared beyond the park at the south end of the avenue.

"Too right, Hy," Colonel Trenchfoot seconded. "The beggar was hosing us down with 50mm soft explosives, probably dum-dums at that. I'd better dig one or two out of the street."

He peered upward to be sure the coast was clear, and hurried off on his errand, returning the Marines' snappy rifle salute with a casual wave of his hand.

"I'm sure," the plump Political Officer commented, speaking for the first time, and still breathing hard from his sprint for safety, "that no hostile intent should be read into the matter. The more especially as we are here to assist in drafting the proposed accord with these confounded Ree!"

"Indeed, Hencrate?" his supervisor queried in a tone of Icy Neutrality (179-C). "It was my impression that the scoundrel deliberately chewed up the antique tilework at my very feet."

"Yeah, but a minute ago you said—" Hencrate blithered.

"I am well aware of what I said, Hencrate," the Ambassador cut him off curtly. "It would be well for your own career development if you would give appropriate attention to my example of idealogical flexibility. A foolish consistency, Henry, is the hobgoblin of little minds," the great man concluded solemnly.

"Hey, you got that last part from whatshisname, uh, Emerson . . . or Thoreau or somebody," Hencrate blurted, with a distinct undertone of one who exposes sham. "Uh, most apropose, too, sir," he added belatedly.

"Apro-poe, Hencrate," the Ambassador corrected. "And I suggest you learn to distinguish between litarary allusion and plagiarism, the better to apreciate the *bon mot.*"

"Bomo?" Hencrate repeated dully.

"He means 'bonn mott,' Henry," Felix interpreted behind his hand. "Means something like 'wisecrack.' "

"By no means, Hy," Magnan demurred. "The translation is more like 'clever saying,' with no connotation of unseemly levity."

Colonel Trenchfoot now returned from his projectile recovery errand.

"Did any of you fellows get the scoundrel's ID number?" he asked dubiously.

"I was *quite* fully occupied, Trenchfoot, in seeking to prevent a fatality in the person of myself," the Political Officer pointed out.

"Selfless, Hencrate," Magnan congratulated his fellow staff member.

"Talking about selfless," Hy Felix said loudly. "How come we're standing around here waiting for the rascal to come back and finish the job? Personally, I say let's get on up to the twelfth floor and leave the body-count to the military boys. Right, Colonel?"

"I see no impropriety in an orderly withdrawal at this juncture, from a military standpoint," Trenchfoot agreed, edging closer to the great glass-slab doors. "In fact," he added, warming to his thesis, "it might legitimately be argued that having drawn enemy fire, thus forcing them to betray their position, it is incumbent upon us to survive so as to report our findings." He opened his hand to reveal two flattened copper-jacketed slugs. "Caliber .082," he stated. "A non-standard load, thus clearly of alien manufacture; Ree manufacture, to be specific."

"We already know that, Colonel," Felix jeered. "Any kid of about seven who builds model aircraft knows a Ree day-fighter when he sees one. What else is new?" Hy snickered, casting a side-long glance Ambassadorward to assess the effect of his remark.

"Cleverly reasoned, I'm sure, Colonel," Sidesaddle conceded, ignoring Felix. "And at considerable personal risk," he added. "I'll see a mention is made in my next dispatch to the Department."

"Could of got us all killed," Hencrate amplified sullenly. "It's OK for *you*, Trenchfoot; you're in the Armed Forces, where they give you medals and stuff. But what would Sector say if they found five Terry diplomatic corpses blocking the walk when they went out for lunch break, hah?"

"Gentlemen!" Ambassador Sidesaddle cut in. "Let me remind you that ours is a mission of peace, not war! Let others expose their reactionary tendencies by over-responsiveness to trivial provocation! As for us, as diplomatic officers charged with maintaining a state of unalloyed chumship with our fellow sentients in the Arm, surely we can refuse to allow ourselves to be distracted by every trifling incident which happens to occur in our vicinity!"

"Oh, well put, sir," Magnan gushed. "And after they shot up your personal spinner, Chief of Mission, For The Use Of, too."

"As to that, Ben," Sidesaddle replied stiffly, "I've a notion a stiff note to the Ree Chargé at Dobe will soon show that scoundrel the error of his ways."

"Ahem, I say, Mr. Ambassador," Hencrate ventured. "Wouldn't that proposal be likely to be misconstrued by some as sheer jingoism?"

"Jingoism, Hencrate?" the Ambassador echoed. "Me? You charge your very own chief with irresponsible sabre-rattling?"

"Not me, Your Excellency," Hencrate protested. "Remember I said 'misconstrued.'"

The further deterioration of Hencrate's career was forestalled for the moment by the abrupt arrival amid a miniature dust cyclone whirled up by its air-cushions, of a fast, black-enamel-with-chrome-inlays dispatch car, Chief, Security Services, For The Use Of, which skidded to a halt athwart the carved curbstone, nearly colliding with the angel fountain.

A pair of CDT security men stepped briskly

from the vehicle almost before it came to rest, and advanced purposefully, briefcases in hand, their expression grim.

"Find out what this is all about, Ben," the Ambassador directed his Econ Officer, stepping back to allow his subordinate to edge forward to intercept the newcomers, who first tried to skirt him, then halted reluctantly and closed ranks to carry on a whispered conference, which Magnan tried vainly to overhear.

"Magnan, CDTO-1, First Secretary of Embassy of Terra at Flamme," the latter introduced himself hastily.

"Cruthers, Foreign Service Inspector," the nearer of the two newcomers said over his shoulder, terminating his conference with obvious reluctance.

"Could I just ask you gentlemen what it is which occasions such haste this fine morning?" Magnan bored on as Cruthers turned his back to snap at his partner. The inspector turned a pained look on Magnan.

"No time for gossip, Mr. Magnan," he said curtly. "I and Sid are already running late; I hear Ambassador Sidesaddle that's supposed to be sitting in on the conference this AM is as temperamental as a Minority Spokesman about being kept waiting. C'mon, Sid." Cruthers brushed past Magnan to find himself confronted by the short, pigeon-shaped physique of Ambassador Sidesaddle himself.

"One moment, Cruthers," he said, holding up an imperious hand. "No need to keep the Ambassador waiting at all. *I* am he."

Sid, peering from behind his colleague's

shoulder, stage-whispered, "Ha! He don't look so tough, Charlie. Show him your badge."

Shushing his helper with a curt motion of his hand, Cruthers assumed a confidential tone:

"Actually, Mr. Ambassador, as you yourself well know, sir, it would be a gross breach of security, as well as of the letter of the Manual, sir, were I to divulge the nature of the information I and Sid are delivering to the Undersecretary."

"No big deal, Charlie," said Sidesaddle smoothly, "just tip me as to what I'm going to run into up there."

"Well, sir, since you've given me a direct order, I must of course defer to your Excellency's exalted rank. Word just came in from Fringe HQ that Space Arm reports no luck all across the board. They've been running a covert search and destroy, and the only Ree units they've seen fired first. So—well, you can see, sir, that leaves the ball in *our* park."

"Our chaps surrendered without a fight?" Colonel Trenchfoot butted in loudly, netting a triple *shussh*! from the Ambassador plus the two inspectors.

"Quiet, Trenchfoot," the Ambassador added curtly. "Inasmuch as we know nothing, officially, of the matter, it would be well if we refrained from leaping to any conclusions pertaining thereto."

"See?" Sid said. "He did it again."

Sidesaddle stepped back, made Alphonse and Gastón motions.

"Don't let me delay you in performance of your duties, gentlemen," he said as if for a Galactic teleview audience. "Magnan, gentlemen, don't block the way."

"Gee, sir," Magnan blurted, "you don't think they've got the entry bugged, do you?"

"Not unless security considerations render such a precaution advisable, in the opinion of those gallant bureaucrats entrusted with responsibility for such measures," Sidesaddle reassured his subordinate, plus anyone who might be monitoring the bug.

"Golly, Ben," Hy Felix put in sympathetically, "His Excellency has got the knack of not saying nothing down to a science, hey?" He wilted at a sharp glance of rebuke from His Excellency.

"Not 'nothing,' Hy," the great man pointed out glacially. "Just the absolute minimum—so as to reduce the likelihood of leaking hot dope to enemy spies, of course."

"Well, what now, gentlemen?" Sidesaddle addressed his underlings as the doors *whoosh!*ed shut behind the inspectors. "It appears certain hotheads have assayed a show of force, but failed to intimidate the insidious Ree. That," he concluded with satisfaction, "leaves matters squarely up to diplomacy, in its pure form. Now, we mustn't keep the Secretary waiting. So, shall we, gentlemen?"

Hy Felix responded by hauling the big black glass door open for the others to file through. Bringing up the rear, Magnan paused to mutter to the Infomation attache.

"One almost wishes Retief were here, eh, Hy?" a gambit which netted him a sour look from the former editor of the Caney, Kansas *Poultryman's Gazette*.

"But he *ain't* here, Ben," Hy grunted. "He's

still taking wildlife census on Icebox Nine or
something, after that fiasco out on Furtheron,
eh? We won't see any more of him fer a while.
Not that he'd make any difference: these here
Ree got the Forces buffaloed, and the Corps,
too. Let's go on up and find out what the Deep-
Think teams have come up with."

2

The VIP conference room in which the his-
toric Peace Strategy Council was to be held was
on the twelfth floor. Three banks of elevators
discharged arriving functionaries from Missions
throughout Tip Sector who, with the profession-
alism of long experience, busied themselves com-
peting for advantageous seats at the long table,
with its mathmatically precisely positioned long
yellow pads and needle-sharp number two pen-
cils at each place.

"The principle, Marvin," senior Cultural Attache Underthurst advised a young General Services Officer, "is to pick a spot close enough to
the head of the table to be able to catch the eye
of the chairman when you need to, but not close
enough to put you directly in his line of vision,
if he's looking for somebody to ream."

"Gosh, thanks, Mr. Underthrust," Marvin Lackluster said, and neatly hooked a chair rung with
his foot just in time to preempt it from occu-
pancy by an over-weight Counselor from the
legation at Moosejaw.

"At the same time, Marvin," his mentor
whispered, taking the adjacent place, "one
mustn't be thoughtless of matters of protocol;

after all, the Moosejaw Cadre may be making out your ER some day."

"Gee whiz, sir," the lad replied. "I didn't realize just coming in and sitting down would be so technical. We didn't learn anything about this part at the short course back at the Department."

"Hist! Here he comes!" Hy Felix's nasal whisper cut across the hubbub from the lookout post he had taken up at the door. At once, silence reigned, as glassy smiles—"Not too frivolous-looking, mind you, Marvin," Underthrust warned —were adjusted in readiness to greet the chairman. Instead, a reedy Admin type came in, and cleared his throat. The profound, attentive silence grew even more profound.

"Gentlemen; you too, Hy," the advance man began, pausing for the academic laugh, while Felix took his seat.

"Gentlemen, as an index of the gravity of today's meeting," the Admin type went on, "no less a personage than Temporary Acting Deputy Undersecretary Crodfoller himself will chair the proceedings."

"Well, it's better'n George, the janitor," Elmer Proudfoot, an Assistant Political Officer, said in the too-loud tone that had so often delayed his career development.

"I heard that, Elmer!" the hoarse voice of the janitor came from the back of the room. Before Elmer could phrase a rejoinder absolving himself of prejudice against custodial personnel, the door swung wide and Undersecretary Crodfoller entered, going directly to his upholstered chair at the head of the table as all hands rose; he replied to the chorus of effusive greeting with a grunt. As he settled himself, his deceptively bland gaze ran along the rows of faces: he summoned his advance man with a jab of a plump thumb.

"Clarence," his glutinus voice sounded clearly, "I thought I told you to weed out the trash first."

"Gee, sir, I was just going to, when you arrived so punctually." Clarence consulted his watch. "Actually, Mr. Temp—er, Act—, er, Depitty Undersecretary, sir," he said boldly. "Your Excellency is twelve seconds early."

"Precisely," Crodfoller pronounced the word as if confirming proof of his infallibility. "Now, down to business, gentlemen." He waved away the hovering Clarence, picked up a pristine pencil, and began drawing interlocking rectangles on his pad.

"Any suggestions from the floor before we begin?" he inquired in a tone which discouraged response. "What about you, Morris?" His little eyes glinted at Ambassador Sidesaddle, who writhed for a moment before rising, having assumed an expression of Astonishment at an Unwarranted Challenge (15-B).

"Whom, I, sir?" he inquired in an ingratiating tone quite at variance with that with which he was accustomed to address his staff. "I?" he repeated. "Why, sir, isolated as I am at Dobe, well off the trade routes, I've had little opportunity to fill myself in on the particular problem—the Ree invasion, I presume you mean, sir."

Crodfoller drew a jagged line across the pattern which had begun to evolve on his pad and wrote, 'Sidesaddle, have record up for review.' Then he let his glance wander to the cadaverous, uniformed figure of General Ralph Otherday.

"Ralph," the chairman addressed the officer blandly, "perhaps you'd be good enough to outline the situation for Ambassador Sidesaddle, and any others present who may have failed to keep their Classified Despatch Binders up to date."

General Otherday rose, a tall, gaunt man with a heavily sunlamped face and a black brush mustache.

"Fellows," he began abruptly. "It's like this: those damn worms—the Ree, they call themselves—have been making nuisances of themselves all across Tip space for some months now. Our intelligence boys say they've strayed across from the Western Arm, and we've been getting howls from every Tom, Dick, and Meyer on the frontier: infernal worms landing and menacing settlers and generally acting as if they own the place—. All our outlying systems are infested, it appears, and with our thin coverage out there, we haven't been able to bring them to decisive battle. One report here—" he stabbed at an imaginary trideogram of Tip space suspended before him "—and the next one over *here*." He indicated a spot eighteen inches, or a fractional light, from the first. "We head out that way, and they strike behind us, just isolated units, you understand, no concentration of force we can get our teeth into. So far, they've nibbled their way halfway across the Tip, and are about to enter the Arm proper. Frankly, we're running low on supplies, and the minor skirmishes we've had so far have been quite indecisive. So—we'll either have to mobilize the reserves, or call for an appropriation that will enable us to mount an across-the-board offensive, *or* fall back to prepared positions within the Arm and wait for their next move."

"Ah, the appropriation you have in mind, General," Crodfoller mused in a tone of innocence. "About how much—"

"Precisely twenty billion GUC this fiscal year, Mr. Undersecretary," the general replied promptly. "Calling up the reserves would be cheaper—and faster."

"Out of the question!" Crodfoller's pronouncement blanketed the chorus of shocked gasps from the committee members.

General Otherday resumed his seat, clipped a Jorgensen cigar, and glanced Chairmanward inquiringly, at which Crodfoller boomed:

"Light that thing, Ralph, and we'll see what kind of job a buck general can do on KP."

The general deftly tucked away the offensive smoke, unlit, and assumed a bitter smile. "Sorry, sir. I'm just a simple soldier, you recall, not accustomed to such plush surroundings, of course. Out there in the foxholes, we get a little careless about the niceties like air-conditioning."

"It's my understanding that you and your staff are quartered at the Ritz-Krudlu, on Gaspierre, Ralph," Crodfoller countered. "Had no intention of denying a vereran his comforts, of course."

"Sure," the general agreed, "but what about these Ree? While we're sitting here jawing about air conditioning, they're eating our outposts and settlements like a Creepie swallowing jelly beans."

"It is precisely that question that brings us here today, Ralph," Crodfoller said reasonably. "I have, at the request of your chief, Grand Admiral Starbird, called together my Principal

Officers and their key staffs from every mission above Consulate-General rank in the entire Sector! And I am now prepared, gentlemen," the Crodfoller glance drifted along the eager faces at the table, "to entertain any constructive proposals which those of you who, unlike Ambassador Sidesaddle, have kept abreast of events, may care to offer."

"What did he say?" Hy Felix asked Colonel Trenchfoot. "I heard him, but I got lost somewhere."

Colonel Trenchfoot *shush*!ed the Press man and cleared his throat.

"As the general said, sir," he addressed Crodfoller, "it's about time we got off our duffs and showed these worms who's running the Arm."

"Ahem, Colonel," the Undersecretary replied, "I can overlook your aggressive terminology because you're new to the give and take of enlightened diplomacy."

"Looks to me like we're doing all the giving, and they're doing all the taking, Boss," Trenchfoot came back cheekily. Hy Felix snickered.

"Mr. Magnan," Crodfoller singled out the inoffensive Econ man for attention, "What have you to contribute at this juncture?"

"Well, sir, if this is a juncture, I feel we should perhaps do something positive."

"*If* this is a juncture, you say, Magnan?" The Undersecretary's frown resembled a cold front forming over jagged mountain peaks. "Inasmuch as I characterized it as a juncture, you wish to question my judgment?" Crodfoller paused ominously and deliberately blacked in a square on his pad, and noted 'Run a 734 on Magnan.'

"Insubordination will contribute little to inter-planetary peace, Ben," he pointed out sadly.

"All I said was—" Magnan began, but was cut off by Crodfoller's booming voice, his face now wreathed in smiles.

"Enough of dissention, fellows," he suggested. "Mr. Lackluster, we haven't yet heard from you."

"Uh, sir, that is, Mr. Assistant Deputy—I mean Deputy Assistant—er, Mr. Undersecretary, that is," Marvin faltered, looking desperately to First Secretary Underthrust for a hint.

"Why don't we just send 'em a blank surren-der form, signed and sealed, and let them fill in the terms?" the older diplomat suggested in a sardonic whisper to his pupil.

"Why don't we—uh, just send 'em a blank surrender form," Marvin parroted, "and let them fill in the terms . . . OK, sir?"

"Oh–kay, Marvin?" Crodfoller echoed hollowly. "When has a fighting Crodfoller ever been known to throw in the figurative towel without a show of symbolic resistance? I'll have no craven proposals, gentlemen! We can achieve the same results while at the same time saving face, if we put on a spirited retreat," he amplified.

"I say, let's form up a cordon and lay for the infernal worms out past Tip space," General Otherday proposed loudly.

"Warmongering, Ralph? *Open* warmongering, at that. I'm surprised at you, General. A bit more subtlety is to be expected of an officer of your rank, even if you *are* known as a hawk type."

"Sir, I can't sit here and let the Armed Forces be slurred," the general stated, rising.

"Otherday, do you mean to stand there and

tell me your service so far lacks resilience as to be unable to accommodate to the realities of inter-Arm relations?"

"As for inter-Arm relations," the general came back doggedly. "The less there is of 'em the better."

"Isolationism?" Crodfoller cried in a tone of Deep Anguish (17-V). "Pardon my use of the expression, gentlemen—but I was *deeply* shocked."

"Maybe we could sort of feint a move to get 'em to raise their picket lines to about the galactic ecliptic level," General Otherday improvised, "and sneak a task force in under them."

"Underarm strategy, General?" Crodfoller, overcome by strong emotion, covered his eyes and moaned. "I see I must reemphasize, gentlemen, that this is a *peace* conference. A unilateral one, to be sure, inasmuch as our overtures through normal channels have been spurned by the Ree—or worse, ignored. What's an Acting Assistant Deputy Undersecretary to do?"

"A *Temporary* Acting Assistant Deputy Undersecretary," someone muttered, an amendment Crodfoller pretended not to hear, merely jotting the word 'Rot' on his pad.

"But I think we all see the problem, now, boys," he went on more spiritedly, sitting up with an air of briskness.

"The time, gentlemen," he stated in tones of Impending Doom (731-W) not unmixed with History in the Making (003-a)* "has arrived: the

*A nuance not listed in the official handbook CDT-628B-1 rev. 6/9/25, but well-known to junior bureaucrats throughout the Corps, said to have been originated by no less a personage than Career Ambassador Spradley on the occasion of his announcement of the Yill-Terry Accord in 479 AE.

time for creative diplomacy on a scale undreamed of by our predecessors."

"Cool, boss," Press Officer Felix murmured, *sotto voce*, "but what's it *mean*?"

"To those who pretend not to recognize the immense significance of this moment," Crodfoller went on, pointedly ignoring Hy's query, though he circled 'Rot' on his pad, "I can say only that History has not, heretofore, presented honest diplomats with such an opportunity to lay the foundation for an unprecedented era of peaceful coexistence."

"*What* kind of diplomats did he say?" Hy inquired of Magnan, his neighbor at the long conference table, nudging Magnan with a shirt-sleeved elbow in solicitation of acceptance of his good-natured jibe.

"Quiet, Hy," Magnan hissed, withdrawing as far as the confines of his chair would permit from any appearance of cronyhood with the notoriously indelicate Press man.

"I think, Ben," the Undersecretary suggested in an ominously mild tone, his gaze fixing on Magnan, "that if you and Hy would postpone your lively exchange until happy hour this evening, I might better be able to convey to the staff the need for immediate and effective action as regards the alleged incursions of the Ree into Terran mandated space."

" 'Alleged,' heck!" Hy said, spoiling the moment of respectful silence the rest of the staff had spontaneously accorded the great man's pronouncement.

"Everybody knows," Hy went on, "the confounded worms have infiltrated Tip space and dispossessed Terry settlers from their homes."

"Hy," Crodfoller said sadly, "I've cautioned you before regarding the use of derogatory epithets directed at alien species!" He eyed Hy without approval. "After all, Hy," he went on, "after we've succeeded in our present effort and have entered with a treaty of eternal chumship with these damned worms, whom I'm sure will settle down to a more halcyon pattern of coexistence once they've been properly pacified and reoriented, such past lapses could rise up to haunt your personnel file."

"Just like not knocking the old-Moosejaw fatso," Marvin whispered over-loudly. "Which I might wind up with him as my supervisor someday, right, Mr. Underthrust?"

"A modicum of discretion, Marvin, might well be in order," Crodfoller suggested. "And I submit that calling Counsellor Lipschitz 'Fatso' is unlikely to contribute to your career development."

"I never meant—" Marvin began, but subsided at a sharp jab in the ribs by his mentor.

"You know, Ben," Ambassador Sidesaddle commented to Magnan behind his hand, "this one is getting off to an even worse start than usual. Half an hour we've been at it already, at combined salaries of maybe fifty thou per hour, and all we've done so far is find out that Space Arm wants more money."

All hands swiveled in shock at the sound of a diffident rapping at the door. Chairman Undersecretary Crodfoller, his wattles a dangerous purplish shade, assumed an expression of Astonishment at a Gaffe of Unprecedented Proportions (1231-p) and grated, "See what they want, George."

The janitor dutifully went to the door, opened

it and was thrust aside by a young fellow in the blues of a Naval rating, holding a strip of gram paper before him as if it were about to burst into flames.

"Par me, fellows," he blurted, "I got some hot poop here the Chief said you wanna see." He looked inquiringly at Crodfoller at the head of the table, then summarized:

"Seems like one of your boys is in deep stuff, Mr. Assis—uh, Deputy . . ."

" 'Mr. Undersecretary' will do, my boy," Crodfoller offered kindly.

"Sure, Mr. Undersecretary, sir," the yeoman agreed, nodding vigorously. "Anyways, we got word here the worms have now took over Region Thirteen. Not a whole lot out there, but according to the records, you got some kinda dog-catcher out on Icebox Nine, which it's in that area, taking a icicle census or like that." The lad guffawed comfortably to indicate that he was essaying a jest.

"To be sure," Crodfoller conceded, nodding in agreement with himself. "Dismissed, my boy."

The yeoman saluted and left.

Crodfoller addressed Magnan,

"I seem to recall something of the matter, a sort of semi-disciplinary thing, wasn't it Ben? Some sort of insubordination charge. I recall you testified in the fellow's favor at the hearings."

Magnan nodded. "Yes sir: not exactly in his favor, sir; just the truth. There *were* extenuating circumstances. Although he *did* leave a Career Ambassador to languish in a Crawlie dungeon for a week or two, he *was* the one who rescued him, otherwise he'd still be in stir or worse."

"Doubtless," the chairman said doubtfully. "In

any case, Ben, it's not wise to allow oneself to be drawn into such matters; tendency to acquire guilt by association, you know."

"Oh, but I *was* associated with him—Retief was his name, Mr. Undersecretary," Magnan pointed out. "Through no fault of my own, we served together at Furtheron and a number of other stations—you remember, he was a third secretary in your mission to Petreac—and actually, I sort of miss him. How long was he supposed to be on detached duty?"

"Oh, a normal hardship post tour, I suppose, perhaps thirteen months standard," Crodfoller replied. "But as I seem to recall, the fellow was something of a chronic trouble-maker, so it's just as well he's out of the way for a time."

"Oh, I was just thinking, Mr. Undersecretary," Magnan said almost wistfully. "Retief used to have a kind of knack for cutting through the formalities and getting down to cases. Unorthodox, of course, but with blank surrender forms under discussion, perhaps we need his unique approach."

"Perish the thought, Ben," the Chairman grunted. "An idea like that is enough to make blank surrender forms seem almost reasonable."

"I suppose so," Magnan agreed, wagging his narrow head in resignation. "Still, we can't very well let one of our own perish miserably at the hands of the aggressors, while we do nothing . . . I hope."

"Certainly not, Magnan. In fact, you yourself may draft a stiff Note, requesting his return in a reasonable time. Nothing truculent, of course. A 'We beings of the world quite understand this

THE RETURN OF RETIEF

sort of thing is bound to occur from time to time' approach."

"Why not send a small destroyer force in there and conduct some maneuvers?" General Otherday proposed.

"Now, General, that's precisely the sort of jingoism we must avoid at all cost!" Crodfoller rebuked the imprudent officer sharply. "Destroyers, indeed! This is the time, gentlemen, for the Corps to show its consummate virtuosity, to continue a reasoned dialog in the face of what lesser persons might consider extreme provocation. But we are not to be provoked! Why, I'm as outraged as anyone; after all, I *did* tell Ben to get out a note—a *stiff* note, only not *too* stiff. If the fellow is still alive, we'll have him back in a year or two, doubtless all the more seasoned for his experience."

"A Ree prison is a pretty dismal place for a Terry to have to spend a night, much less a year or two," Hy Felix commented, jotting a note on his pad. "Cells are two foot by two foot, and four foot high," he added. "Kinda cramped for a six-footer plus."

"Now, Hy, I want no imprudent press releases on this matter before I've had time to think through my responses," Crodfoller commanded. "Not that I'd dream of attempting to muzzle the press, of course. Still, you'd do wise to heed my admonition. By the way, how long do you have to go for retirement? Only another year or two, eh?"

"Right, boss," Hy agreed. "But what's that got to do—"

"He only means if you should understandably drag your feet a little, the matter will fade out

and no need to upset anybody, eh, chief?"
Magnan interpreted.

"Any inquiry arising from imprudent disclo-
sures would certainly tend to hold major personnel actions such as retirements in abeyance, was
what I had in mind, Hy," Crodfoller explained
kindly. "If you don't kick a dead mudrat, it'll
never stink," as my old grandpa used to say,"
he amplified genially.

"Sure, sir," Magnan blurted. "But what are
we going to do about Retief? While we're sitting
here, he's rotting in a worm holding cell in
Iceberg Nine. He could die of pneumonia before
we get there!"

"Get there, Magnan?" Crodfoller queried
glacially. "You forget, Ben, I have already counselled a measured response to this no doubt
accidental breach of diplomatic privilege."

"Mr. Undersecretary," General Otherday spoke
up, "this may be precisely the opportunity for
which Space Arm has been longing: if the
damned worms have committed themselves to
an occupation in force of this region, I can put a
cordon around them and bottle them up tighter
than Dick's hatband after he washed it, once the
appropriation goes through, that is."

Crodfoller abruptly rose to his feet, toppling
his chair on its back, where its hip-u-matic swivel
attachment caused it to thresh like a stricken
thing. "Have I fallen among out-and-out war-
mongers?" the chairman yelled. "Am I to hear
nothing but proposals for genocide? Are we
diplomats, or are we barbarians?"

"What we are, boss," Hy Felix offered in the
stricken silence, "what we are is a bunch of
paperpushers, let's face it. Ben, if your old pal

Retief got himself in this fix on his own, he'll have to get out the same way."

"Precisely my point, Hy," Crodfoller said quickly. "And don't you worry about the old retirement."

"Marvin," Underthrust whispered urgently to the neophyte, "did you see how quickly his Ex checked over his possible response spectrum, and selected a winner? Hardly paused. Magnificent!"

"Yessir," Lackluster confirmed enthusiastically, "I noticed his face writhing a little, when he tried on a 602 Indignation, then a 431 Reluctant Satisfaction with a Subordinate's Performance."

"Still," Magnan persisted, with a slight quaver, "I think perhaps we have a sort of obligation, almost, in a sense, to attempt—to state an intention to try to attempt, that is—some kind of affirmative action to show these worms they can't just invade Terry-mandated space and capture harmless Terry bureaucrats." He sat down abruptly.

"I hope I didn't express myself too vigorously, Your Excellency," he added. "Perhaps I got a little carried away."

"By no means, Ben," Crodfoller said kindly. "Actually, I admire your spirited efforts in support of a colleague—a junior, at that— no matter how he himself may have contributed to the present contretemps."

"*He* contributed to it, sir?" Magnan echoed. "How? All he did was go where he was assigned."

"Indeed, Ben? Are you quite sure he voiced no resentment when he found himself overwhelmed by an unauthorized invasion of aliens?"

"Why, no, sir," Magnan quavered. "As to that,

why, I suppose perhaps he might well have expressed some objection."

"So you see?" Crodfoller beamed along the board. "No need overly to excite ourselves, gentlemen, though I *shall* look into the matter one day soon, when other, more substantive matters have been dealt with. For example, just how we can best indicate to the Ree, without giving offense, that our plans for development of the region do not include the settlement of hordes of displaced persons from the Western Arm?"

"I still say let's show 'em a little muscle," Colonel Trenchfoot muttered doggedly. "Not an actual attack, if that's too rich for your blood, but just show the flag, like, with a goodwill tour of Tip space by the Second Fleet, maybe."

"Threats of force, Trenchfoot, I repeat," Crodfoller intoned stonily, "are hardly the finest expression of enlightened diplomacy."

"To heck with 'threats of force,' " Hy grumped. "How's about going directly to force, and no threats to tip 'em off."

"These reactionary comments, Mr. Felix," the Undersecretary stated formally, "reflect little credit on the Information Agency you represent in these councils."

"I'm speaking for myself," Hy said bluntly. "The Agency's just as chicken as the Corps—maybe more so."

"In that case, Hy, give me a break," Crodfoller demanded. "Don't file a story on the negotiation until after the apparent conflict of interest has been resolved. Why, I imagine that when tempers have cooled, and counsels of restraint have prevailed, you'll be very glad indeed that

you didn't go on record with any premature
pronouncements possibly critical of Corps policy."

"File what?" Hy demanded. "A first-grade spell-
ing bee'd make hotter copy than this get-to-
gether."

The subdued hubbub which followed Felix's
gaffe had hardly died down when again the de-
liberations of the august body were interrupted
by a rap at the door. Grumpily, Crodfoller turned
to rebuke the intruder, but the reprimand died
on his lips as he was greeted by the entrance of
a tall, broad-shouldered man clad in a scorched
and torn garment barely recognizable as a CDT
issue coverall, informal, undeveloped worlds, for
use on, and supporting on one shoulder a bulky
polyon bag.

"What's this, sir?" Crodfoller barked. "Your
appearance is disgraceful!"

"Not nearly as disgraceful as his *dis*appearance,
Mr. Undersecretary," Magnan objected, jumping up excitedly. "Retief," he went on more
calmly, addressing the newcomer, "we'd heard
you'd been captured by the insidious Ree, out
on Icebox Nine!"

"Not quite, Mr. Magnan," Retief replied coolly.
"I spotted them landing, and decided to surround them, just in case."

"Surround them?" Crodfoller echoed hollowly.
"You did nothing to create an impression of
hostility, I hope!"

"Nothing much, Mr. Undersecretary," Retief
demurred. "I just gave them a good scare, and
let it go at that."

"Indeed? And how, may I ask, did you, a single individual, terrorize an entire detachment of
Ree?"

"Easy," Retief said, as he seated himself and dumped on an adjacent chair the polyon bag he was carrying.

"A small Ree VIP scout-boat landed in an adjacent sector," he reported. "Captain Fump, who seemed not only lost but at his wit's end, pulse-bombed my bubble and sent a squad after me. I dodged the squad, boarded the scout, and parleyed with Captain Fump."

"Oh, dear; oh, dear," Crodfoller mourned. "A VIP boat, you say; and you waylaid the VIP himself. I do hope you didn't give offense. A complaint lodged by an important Ree dignitary just at this juncture could prove disastrous to my plans for a Ree-Terry accord."

"Don't sweat, Mr. Undersecretary," Retief soothed the great man. "Captain Fump didn't complain. He got interested in my gun collection, and hardly uttered a word."

"How did you get here, Mr. Retief?" Crodfoller demanded. "All unessential travel has been suspended for the duration of the crisis." The Undersecretary pulled at his ear thoughtfully. "And it was my understanding you had been delivered to Icebox Seventeen or whatever by a Corps lighter, which at once returned to base. You, I believe, were to await pick-up at the conclusion of your assignment, some months hence."

Retief nodded. "I had to take Fump's boat," he explained. "Unfortunately, it got shot up a little on the way in."

"Worse and worse," Crodfoller mourned. "You had the audacity to preempt, confiscate, requisition—"

"Steal is the word you want," Retief put in. "Yep. I did. Steal Fump's boat, I mean."

"And then permitted the borrowed vessel to be damaged by an alert Naval Patrol," Crodfoller grieved.

"Not quite," Retief corrected. "Our alert patrols weren't around. Did you forget? Today is the Inter-Arm Friendship Ceremonial. All patrols are grounded for Maximum Fraternization. It was a Ree Dreadnought that opened fire on me."

"This," Crodfoller pronounced, "is disaster, unadorned. It's war, Mr. Retief! And *you* precipitated it." Hastily the Undersecretary scribbled out a whole row of squares.

"No, just a routine foul-up," Retief corrected. "After all, the Ree fired on a Ree boat by mistake; no official Terran involvement at all."

"Let us hope," Crodfoller said fervently, "that Captain Fump is sufficiently large-minded to view the affair in that light."

"A fast Note of Apology ought to do the trick," the long-silent political officer Proudfoot suggested quickly, thereby scoring a point for anticipating his colleagues, a coup which the Undersecretary duly noted on his pad: 'Proudfoot—1 up.'

"Why don't we just send along a few billion GUC as a sort of subsidy or something?" Hencrate wondered aloud.

"What?" Colonel Trenchfoot barked. "Pay tribute to these pirates, when they haven't even demanded any?"

"That's far the best time, Colonel," Ambassador Sidesaddle pointed out, almost kindly. "This way *we* get to set the amount of the reparations," he finished, pointedly avoiding the word 'tribute.'

"Yeah," Marvin Lackluster blurted, "but what

are we paying reparations for?" The young fellow scratched his scalp, miming Honest Confusion (32-b).

"Marvin," the Undersecretary said gently, "don't waste that rather unsophisticated 32 on this simple question. After all, when offered ten or twelve billion GUC in amends, are the Ree likely to query the philosophical basis of the grant?"

"But it was Mr. Retief who got shot at," Marvin persisted, at which the Undersecretary noted, 'Lackluster—stubborn' on his crowded pad.

"Quick action is essential, gentlemen," the Undersecretary rapped out in his most authoritative tone, a modified 738-z (Patience Reluctantly Prodded to Stern Action). "Initially, of course, I must prepare a formal apology to Captain Fump, for the signature of the Deputy Undersecretary himself.

As if to refresh himself, Crodfoller took a deep breath and surveyed a yet-untapped sector of the conference table.

"Manny," he prompted, fixing a steely gaze on his Communications Officer, who had been contentedly resting on his oars, "What's our best mode for a fast contact with this confounded worm troublemaker, 'Our esteemed colleague,' that is to say?"

The officer, who had allowed his eyes to glaze, blinked and offered, "Well, sir, with all travel out for the duration like you said, I guess we better get off a quick flash on the hot-line—only it's broken down, I hear."

"If it's broken down, how the heck are we

going to get off any flashes, hot or otherwise, on it?" Crodfoller demanded.

"You've definitely got a point there, Mr. Acting, uh, Assistant Deputy, sir," Manny conceded forthrightly. "I was just coming to that."

"Maybe," a heretofore silent Political Section type from the Consulate at Dobe hazarded, "maybe we'd better try to get the word through via the Groaci Minister at Prute. He's handling Terry affairs out there vis-a-vis the Ree."

" 'Maybe,' Eustance?" the Undersecretary queried. "Do you intend that to be a firm proposal?"

Eustace protested, "I only said—I mean, I was noodling. Why not shove it into the reactor and see if it melts the rods?"

General Otherday rose. "Gentlemen, I predict that Fleet orders declaring a Red Alert Status are even now being issued. Thus I will make every effort to see that my command is on a war footing. Action must not be delayed."

"Swell, General," Crodfoller acceded with a sour-sweet smile, his personal modification of the time-hallowed 29-c (Toleration of the Intolerable in the Interest of Chumship). "But," he went on, "just what is this action you contemplate?"

"I figure to have my Supply Sergeant stock up on smokes and ammo and stuff," the general replied. "No telling how bad the rationing will be."

"There is that," Crodfoller agreed sagely, noting on his pad 'See Mel re essentials.' "But even before that we must, I say MUST, gentlemen, proffer appropriate balm to the wounded Ree ego. We—Mr. Retief, that is—have, or has, offered an affront which will doubtless, as the general suggests, elicit a maximum response from the confounded worms. After all, until now, they have met with nothing but sweet reasonableness, unless you want to count the abortive efforts at interference which General Otherday attributes to our extended patrol units, and even so, their response has been less than conciliatory. Presented with the outrage to Captain Fump, I shrink from contemplating the repercussions. The apology must be made at once!"

On the last words, his voice broke, as did his pencil point as he attempted to jot a note. Then he looked up, his reddened eye falling in turn on each underling sitting slumped along the table. "Are there any, ah, less-than-totally-idiotic proposals, gentlemen?"

"I have one, which might qualify, Mr. Undersecretary," Retief spoke up, netting a glare like a fish-spear from the Undersecretary.

"And what might it be, sir?" Crodfoller grated in an ominous tone.

"Why not tell him yourself?" Retief suggested, as he unknotted the thong securing the lumpy sack beside him. He upended the container, and dumped onto the chair a blunt cylindrical mass which, the assembled diplomats judged from its restless writhing, was a living creature.

3

"Whoof, Retief," a gluey voice issued from the alien, which was decorated on its upper endplate with a complex pattern of orifices and tentacular growths, from which the sound came. "Bagging me up was a pretty cheeky thing to do, you know—" the complaint was interrupted by a muffled sneeze. "Dusty in that spud sack, too," the alien continued.

"I seem to recall that at the time you were quite enthusiastic about it, Fump," Retief pointed out. "But I didn't bring you here to talk about all those promises you made when you were begging me to bag you instead of scragging you."

"A moment," the Undersecretary interrupted. "You suggest, Mr. Retief, that the captain was placed in that rather informal container at his own request?"

"Actually, I stated it quite definitely, Mr. Undersecretary," Retief corrected.

"Why in Tophet would he make such a request?" Crodfoller demanded incredulously.

"Because it was better'n getting recycled with the rest of the garbage," the alien pointed out.

"And why, my dear captain, did you imagine yourself faced with such a Draconian choice?"

"That," Retief spoke up, "was because I was aiming my gun at him with one hand and holding the bag open with the other. He reached his decision quite promptly."

"I bet there's some kind of rule against that," the alien ventured. "A CDT rule, I mean. Us Rees are practical about stuff like that."

"Don't make a speech right now, Fump," Retief cut in. "Undersecretary Crodfoller has something to say to you, I think."

"Sure, I heard," Fump said impatiently, "the sucker wants to offer me a bribe to put the hush on the outrage you slipped over on my boys and me. Go ahead, Herky."

"Uh, you know my name, Captain Fump," Crodfoller responded in a surprised tone.

"Sure, our Confidential Source boys are on the ball," the Ree dignitary confirmed. " 'Hercules Crodfoller'; how could a guy forget a handle like that?"

"I'm flattered, Captain," Crodfoller said shyly. "One was unsure that one's reputation had been noised so far abroad."

"Don't close out your memoirs just yet," Fump cautioned. "I found your name in a pamphlet entitled *Reliables in Event of Ree Occupation of Tip Space*. A list of easy marks, you know, Herky."

"I must protest, Mr, ah, just what *is* your civil title?"

"I'm a Maker of Ritual Grimaces, First Class, in the reserves," the alien replied. " 'Captain' is my regular honorific. Retief calls me 'Fumpy': I like it. Short and snappy, even if it does sound like some kinda Terry handle; no offense. Or maybe a little offense at that." Fump's sense-organ cluster hardened. "I overheard you boys talking about reparations and all. You can hand over the blank surrender forms now, and the fifty million Guck, too."

"Why, the audacity of the fellow fairly takes my breath away," the Undersecretary said in admiring tones to Ben Magnan, who was now standing behind Retief's chair. "And before I could lodge my protest at his implication, too."

"You don't deny the Efficiency Rating of our agents, do you? It was them as made up the Questionnaire and slid it into the system. According to the Form X-13 questionnaire you filled in—*and* signed—you're ready to pay up and shut up, if anybody jumps out and says boo! to you."

"I thought the X-13 was a personnel form I was completing," Crodfoller protested. "I felt I

handled some of the trick questions rather
cleverly. I assumed it was a new technique for
weeding out, if you'll pardon the expression,
isolationists. Like the sneaky one in the 'Ability
to Empathize With Our Friends We Haven't Met
Yet' column: "If you should discover local employees in collusion with black marketeers
(individualist entrepreneurs, that is) to loot the
Embassy commissary, would you (select one):

   "Clobber them and ask questions later
   Request a cut
   Demand a cut
   Call for help
   File a confidential report
   Lodge an official protest
   Fire them en masse (local employees only)
   Volunteer to serve as lookout
   Congratulate them on their enterprise
   None of the above?"

   "I spotted that one easy," Crodfoller continued.
"Transparently bait to tempt one to an intemperate response. But if it was actually a fake,
slipped into channels by Ree espionage agents—
heavens! I shudder to contemplate the impression—"

   "Sure; you can skip all that jazz, Herky," the
cylindrical alien dismissed Crodfoller's complaint. "Us Rees are practical. So let's get down
to cases: are you boys going to turn your backs
and let us deserving underprivileged fellows from
the Western Arm take over East Arm, or what?"

   "Such presumption!" Magnan ventured cautiously, one eye on the Undersecretary's reaction.
Seeing none, he went on: "As if we'd sit back
and allow our brave Terry pioneers in Tip Space
to perish for want of the support they were

promised when we were pushing the *Take a Trip to the Tip* program."

"Now, Ben, I wouldn't precisely say 'promised,'" Crodfoller demurred. "Actually, we said 'maybe, depending on the exigencies of Corps policy' and like that. Check the wording; I'm sure you'll find nothing to which we could actually be rigorously held."

"Anyway, it's a darn shame, just like Ben says," Hy Felix spoke up from his spot downtable. "Our folks have just about had time to start getting a little return on all the time and effort they've put into this Settlement venture—and all of a sudden they got these worms coming in and throwing them off the farm, or worse."

"The Corps," the Undersecretary said loftily, "can hardly assume responsibility for the success of private ventures embarked upon by rootless adventurers."

"Ten years ago we were blanketing the media with our Settlement promo. I know. Remember I've been in journalism a while. Back in Caney, even, we run ads for new breeds of amphibious Plymouth Rocks and fancy hummingbird-ostrich hybrids 'suitable for Frontier conditions.' "

"That's neither here nor there, Hy," Crodfoller dismissed the protest. "As for you, Ben, I'm surprised at such intemperate utterances from a proven bureaucrat of your experience."

"Maybe Hy's bitch ain't here nor there," the alien put in, in his squeaky voice. "But *I'm* here, and I wanna be there, so what are you boys going to do about a little repatriation with apologies, for openers?"

"Why, Captain," Crodfoller replied soothingly (19-r), "I shall of course set wheels in motion at once. As for the apology, I trust an appropriate expression of regret at secretarial level will suffice?"

"I'll settle for half a billion guck and no hypocritical Foreign Office Notes, thanks, Herky," the cocky alien corrected.

"Right away, Captain," Crodfoller agreed quickly. "Oh, Mr. Ambassador," he addressed Sidesaddle, "check with Clarence over at Budget and Fiscal, if you will, and arrange for a draft on counterpart funds."

"Nix, no checks," the alien countered.

"Do you imply, Captain," the Undersecretary challenged in a tone of Icy Outrage, Restrained Only by Superior Moral Fiber, (225-w) "that the CDT would tender a defective instrument in satisfaction of a debt of honor?"

"What's honor got to do with it, bub?" Fump responded in an adamant tone which all hands recognized as an attempt at a classic You Better Loosen Up, Chums, Because I Ain't Giving a Inch (9-a). "After all," the alien continued reasonably, "it's just a case of who's got the power, right?"

As Crodfoller spluttered, unable at once to formulate a reply which would stand scrutiny in light of both Section 9 of CDTM (the Subtleties of Chumship) and Section 42 (Culpable Negligence in Defense of Corps Prestige), Retief took the opportunity to make a comment to the great man.

"Mr. Undersecretary, I suggest you tread delicately at this point. The Ree have only two basic stances in their alien contacts: if they see they're clearly overmatched, they're servile; if they think they have the upper hand, they turn arrogant."

"Arrogant is it, Mr. Retief?" Crodfoller echoed, turning his ire in relief on this handy target. "I remind you, sir, the loose employment of pejoratives anent developing, er emergent, ah, that is, dammit, inferior species is a gross violation of Section 9!"

"Very likely, Mr. Undersecretary," Retief agreed. "But I think I'd better have a few words in private with Fump before he takes title to the entire Arm." With that, Retief shook open the sack in which the Ree had arrived, and over protest both from the alien and from the Terran diplomats present, returned the squat being to its dusty depths, whence he uttered threats mixed with sneezes, until Retief banged the bag smartly against the chair.

"That does it, Mr. Retief!" the outraged Undersecretary yelled, coming to his feet. "As of this moment, sir, you are reassigned to General Services, where you will have responsibility for the filling of semi-annual requisitions from missions in the field, now some three months, standard, in arrears, due to excessive workload and inadequate intellectual capacity on the part of GS personnel, of whom you are now one!"

"Are you forgetting, sir?" Magnan put in hesitantly, "Retief hasn't yet finished his ice-cube census."

Magnan wigwagged for Retief's attention. "I say—that is—what about food? How long can Fump exist in a diplomatic pouch?"

"He estivates," Retief replied. "He needn't be

awakened until the situation is resolved. Oh, by the way," he added, "his minion Goop is estivating in the scout-boat. Farewell, gentlemen. Keep the old CDT flag flying."

4

It was hardly a CDT socio-economic audit period later that Undersecretary Crodfoller summoned Magnan to the Presence. After curtly ordering his underling to be seated, the Undersecretary fixed the mild-mannered Consul and First Secretary with a steely look.

"See here, Ben," he barked. "What's gone wrong at General Services? There's a foul-up in our Goodies for Undesirables program. I have a stack of complaints an inch thick, from Missions in Tip Space mostly, regarding non-receipt of vital emergency supplies. Space Arm swears convoys have been getting through on schedule. The foul-up is clearly here at Sector! What are you doing about it?"

"Me, sir?" Magnan cried in a voice with a tendency to slip into a falsetto. "Gracious, Mr. Dep—er, Assis—er, Acting Undersecretary, why ask *me*? Why, I'm on the Groaci Desk, as your Excellency is aware."

"Um," Crodfoller grunted, a monosyllable well known to his subordinates in the Corps, and commonly translated: "I'm not interested in excuses: better come up with something useful if you expect to salvage your career, such as it is."

"I seem to recall," the Undersecretary went on with the ponderous insistence of a glacial advance, "that you once mentioned that you and this fellow Retief are cronies."

"Not cronies, sir," Magnan objected. "Chums, possibly, or associates, perhaps. That is, we've shared assignments to a number of the most dismal hardship posts in the sector. Not my doing, of course: doubtless Personnel can explain it."

"I'm not conferring with Personnel at the moment, Ben," Crodfoller pointed out coldly. "I'm interviewing you. Ergo, it is you I shall have to depend upon for any answers that are to be forthcoming."

"But—but, sir, what sort of snafu am I supposed to answer for?" Magnan queried in bewilderment.

"In place of sorely needed rubber stamps, red tape, and blank forms, our beleaguered frontier posts are receiving personal armament kits! How are our hard-working bureaucrats to keep their paperwork flowing smoothly in the face of alien invasion without the most basic of supplies?"

"Well, sir," Magnan mused. "Maybe they could sort of spring a little April Fool surprise on the worms when they come swaggering in—"

"Worms, Mr. Magnan, or, ah, Ree troops, that is, do not swagger. I remember that Fump fellow; it was all the begger could do to stand erect! And as for April Fool's Day, Ben: your file is up for review by the Promo Board soon, is it not?"

"Sure, sir, but it wasn't I who shipped guns in place of gummed labels, PAPA gear instead of paper; it was Retief."

"Do you realize, Ben," Crodfoller thundered, a shade more kindly, Magnan estimated hopefully, "that while passing classified comm gear into a hostile world under duty-free entry as 'office supplies' is a time-honored custom, to smuggle in small arms instead could not only jeopardize this convenient polite fiction, at which all sides wink, but could suggest to the Ree that our expressed desire for peace at a reasonable discount is a mere ruse!''

"I guess so, sir," Magnan conceded. "But I'm sure Retief didn't mean any harm—''

"Since the fellow was undoubtedly instrumental in the fiasco," Crodfoller intoned. "It is only meet that he should be given the opportunity to undo the mischief. Accordingly, I am assigning him as Special Envoy to the Ree Legation at Goldblatt's World, one of those which were the victim not only of Ree agression, but of Retief's mismanagement of requisitions! I am informed that no less a Ree dignitary than Chief Intimidator of Insolent Upstarts Slive himself is Chief of Mission there; our man will treat directly with Slive, to convince His Excellency that the CDT is indeed a pacific service, dedicated to cementing cordial relations with all our friends we haven't met yet."

"That seems a rather dirty detail, Mr. Undersecretary," Magnan protested mildly.

"Indeed, Ben? Rather, it is an instance of unsurpassed magnanimity. Let me tell you a story, Ben, concerning an ancestor of mine, General Lord Crodfoller, in command of the Twenty-third Foot at Gheewallah; in Inja, don't you know. According to family tradition, it was during a hot exchange with a well-organized besieging force of hill tribesmen that a young subaltern broke under fire and fled the field. Disgraced, he skulked in his tent, shunned by the Officer's

Mess, and thus doomed to slow starvation. Magnanimously, General Lord Crodfoller summoned the unfortunate fellow, and handed him a dispatch for his subordinate across the valley. All the young fellow had to do to redeem himself was mount and ride across the battlefield in the face of the enemy. Instead, he went to his tent and shot himself. Sad ending, that. I don't suppose Retief is the suicidal type?"

"Oh, no, sir. At least, I don't think—" Magnan stammered.

"You'll find out when you inform him," Crodfoller said shortly.

"M-me, sir?" Magnan said, appalled.

"Yes, better the news comes from a colleague. Of course, the assignment has gone through channels and all that. You, Magnan, are the last to know. Or rather, the next to last. Go and enlighten Retief."

Magnan sighed and tottered away.

Chapter Two

Jerry, the barman at the VIP snack bar, paused after placing a bumper of bacchus black before Retief, and plied his bar-rag vigorously on a nonexistent ring on the polished vermilion heowood.

"Say, Mr. Retief," he blurted at last, "I want to give you my sympathy on your new assignment; hope I'm not getting out of line."

"There's no line waiting to congratulate me, Jerry," Retief reassured the mixologist. "By the way, what new assignment is that?"

"Oh, didn't you hear?" Jerry responded. "All the scuttlebutt has it the Secretary picked you to go out to try and calm down old CIIU Slive, the Ree big shot. I wouldn't want to put my neck into a noose like that, even for a three-grade bump, which I don't guess you'll get."

"If the boys in the latrine know all this, the news ought to be filtering down to First Secretary level pretty soon," Retief commented.

He took his Bacchus black and sauntered toward the kidney-shaped keowood booths. VIP's of all shapes and sexes were cozying up in strategic huddles on the soft, bisque-colored cushions. Pale lanterns hung from the dark, sculptured, sound-absorbent ceiling, diplomatically refraining from throwing too much light.

He found an empty booth, sank onto the cushions, and swirled the Bacchus potion.

"Oh, Retief, there you are," the voice of Mr. Magnan cut across the murmur of well-bred conversation in the lounge. Retief looked up and saluted his immediate supervisor with raised glass.

"Mr. Magnan, here I am indeed," Retief greeted the slightly-built senior diplomat. "But according to Jerry, not for long."

"Ah, yes, Retief," Magnan muttered, as he sat in the booth, "I might have known the bartenders would get the news first. I'm afraid you're being sent as Special Envoy to the Ree Legation at Goldblatt's world. Slive is Chief of Mission there, you know. You're to convince him of our peaceful intentions."

"I'm not the best man for the job," Retief said.

"I know. I mean, none of us deserves Slive. I'm really sorry. But after the fashion in which you aroused the Undersecretarial ire by the indignities you imposed on that nasty little worm, Captain Fump, or whatever, I can hardly say I'm surprised. Still," he went on, "I wish you the best of luck. Do keep in touch. And now I must be off to a mummy-viewing at the Hoogan Legation. Ta."

Magnan got up abruptly and hurried away.

Retief savored his bumper to the last drop, rose, and carried the empty mug to the bar.

"Geeze," Jerry offered, discarding the mug, "you're taking it good, Mr. Retief. Most of the boys would be crying into their beer at an assignment to Goldblatt's. They're really trying to put it to you, Retief. Hang in there. If you let them run you out of the Corps, I'll have to start learning Wormspeak."

2

It had been a spartan three standard day trip out, aboard the rusting tramp freighter which had been the only transport available for the final leg of the long crossing from Aldo to Prute, where Retief was scheduled for initial contact with Ree officialdom via Snith, the Groacian Consul.

"Say, Mr. Retief," the whiskery First Officer said to his lone passenger at dinner on the last night out, "do you or any of them CDT big shots back at Sector meet this Snith, before they go making plans?"

"Only via screen, Big," Retief replied as he sampled the baked Alaska.

"Not too bad, considering, hey, Mr. Retief?" Big suggested, eyeing the desert. At Retief's querying glance, he elucidated:

"Considerin it's been froze, and then scorched," the old spacehand explained apologetically. "Autochef must be on the blink."

"That's all right, Big; it's supposed to be frozen and then scorched," Retief pointed out. "The trick is to brown the meringue without melting the ice-cream inside; and I see the chef almost managed it," he added, as a stream of murky fluid drained out through a hole in the stiff sponge-cake outer layer. "But tell me about Mr. Snith. Do you know him well?"

"About as good as you can get to know a guy who keeps a couple Haterakan meat-hawks chained to their perch beside the legation door. I hafta go up there every trip to hand over the invoices and pick up the bills of lading, and all I ever got was a quick look at the little mother inside his limousine his chauffeur was practically running me down with. But I heard plenty. The boys say he hates Terries worser'n he does the Pruties, which he peppers with buckshot on sight."

"Is he on good terms with the Ree?" Retief asked.

"Better'n with us Terries, I guess," Big offered. "Haven't heard of him shooting at none of them yet, even when they came waltzing into his legation compound, armed to the mandibular serrations."

"Flexible animosity is an old Groaci technique," Retief pointed out. "Thanks for the briefing, Big. How soon do we hit atmosphere?"

"About an hour, I guess," Big supplied crisply. "Better get your stuff aboard the drop-boat— if you're sure you want to go down there. Remember, aside from your pal Snith, you got the Pruties to deal with. Ever met one?"

Retief nodded. "At a cocktail party back at Flamme. Enormously fat fellow, Assistant Grimacer as I recall, bucking for promotion to field grade. Not too different from us single-skulled, bipedal Terries, except for large teeth and a number of muscular arms. Nearly beat me at Drift."

"Bet he cheated, Retief," Big suggested. "I happen to know you're Drift champ for the whole Arm."

"Yes, maybe he cheated a little," Retief acknowledged. "He used three arms. A point for the philosophers. But he was a sore winner; wanted a rematch to prove he could do it with two."

"And you using only one," Big commiserated. "It don't pay to try and play fair with all these here Eeties. They got no conscience. Oops," the mate interrupted himself as a sudden impact shook the vessel.

"That's atmosphere, Retief," he explained unnecessarily as the vessel settled down to a steady buffeting. "Drop boat away in four minutes," he added and hurried off.

3

The Prute Customs and Immigration shed was a squat structure assembled from scraps of corrugated styrene, dim-lit by a hanging jar of Slovian juice-bugs which shed a wan, greenish glow on the deeply-creased olive-hued visage of the Excise Officer who leaned on Retief's locker, foot, junior officers, for the use of, and said:

"I don't care what the treaty says, Bub, it's what *I* say that counts. And I say you pay up in cash or the luggage don't clear Customs this year."

"I suggest you get several of your elbows off my box, Mister," Retief said, and jerked the support from beneath the joints to which he had referred, causing the functionary to collapse like the empty barracks-bag he resembled.

"Hey!" he yelled from the floor, "Grab that Terry! He assaulted me in the performance of my duties!"

"I wouldn't," Retief suggested as a second tax-collector moved in confidently. The Prutian paused and arranged his puckered features in a passable version of the classic What's This, Impertinence? (17-g).

"Precisely," Retief confirmed the query inherent in the alien's features, which resembled the mouth of a sack secured by a drawstring.

"You can't get away with the rough stuff," the newcomer pointed out mildly as he leaned to assist his colleague to his large, flat feet.

"See, we not only got the regs on our side, we also got you outnumbered, wise guy," the latter pointed out as he resumed his position behind the Customs table, this time keeping his elbows out of play.

"Wrong," Retief said. "According to treaty, the personal effects of diplomatic personnel are to be accorded duty-free entry. As for having me outnumbered, how many more boys have you got on call? I only see ten." He picked up the locker and proceeded past the Customs sign to Health and Immigration, where he was confronted by a larger and plumper-than-average Prutian in a heavily braided uniform.

"I'm Chief Inspector Thise," the official stated firmly as Retief paused before him. "Health OK? No fallen arches or ruptures? Got to watch these infectious maladies. An alien microbe could sweep through Prute like wildfire. Caught a Groaci last year with crossed eyes, and considering the little devils have got five eyes, on stalks at that, you can see what the plague could of done to us single vision folks."

"Sounds bad," Retief agreed. "I don't suppose a touch of boredom would constitute much of a threat, would it?"

"Boredom!" the inspector echoed in tones of horror. "We're highly susceptible! Keep back! Don't breath on anything, while I go fetch the medical inspector!"

"Sorry," Retief returned. "I'll have to bend the regs slightly. Breathing is a habit I don't intend to kick."

"We've got a regimen where we can put you on carbon monoxide and taper you off in a couple days," the Prutian countered. "Think of it! Free at last from the simian on your back! You'll thank Prute for the cure once it's done. Don't worry, the withdrawal symptoms only last a short while."

"You don't understand," Retief said. "My mission requires that I stay alive long enough to put a bug in the ear of CIIU Slive. But first I have to see the Groaci Consul here on Prute. So why not simplify matters by calling me a cab and accepting this modest token of my esteem?" He handed over a ten-Guck note which was whisked out of sight at once.

"Say, you wouldn't try to bribe a Prutian official, would you, Terry?" the official mumbled.

"How much do you go for?" Retief inquired interestedly.

"You trying to *buy* me?" the Prutian gasped.

"No; just renting," Retief explained.

"Oh. OK. Don't ever try to buy a official of the great Prutian nation," the local warned. "We run high: sweepers get ten thou, and as fer a Chief Inspector, like me—" the Chief paused to indicate the rank badge on his sleeve. "We start at half a mil."

"Then ten Guck would hardly be considered a genuine bribe," Retief suggested.

"Heck, no!" the alien confirmed. "More like a token of a fella's esteem."

"Fine. Now about that cab," Retief said. "I'd prefer one with a seat and a roof."

"No sweat," the inspector replied. "By the way, you weren't planning on immigrating, I suppose?"

"Not just yet," Retief confirmed.

"So that takes care of that," the inspector said as he deposited an impressive, folded news-paper-sized document in the refuse container. "Say, Terry—er, Mr. Retief, I mean—if you're interested in a little companionship, I got a cou-ple hot numbers."

Retief declined the offer, and was halfway to the exit when a third inspector, this one a bulky chap in civvies, strolled into his path and held up a peremptory hand.

"It's OK that you rolled over Clarence and Rocky," he intoned, "but I'm civilian chief Gluck. So let's see what you got in the lock-box."

"Better move over," Retief replied. "I'm run-ning behind schedule, and I see my cab's here."

"Don't get in too big a hurry, Terry!" Gluck snapped, signalling for a pair of armed guards who moved into position flanking the Terran. "I've got to satisfy myself you ain't carrying contraband." He turned to address the cop, "Open it up."

One of the two policemen took a step toward

the object of official interest. Retief put out an arm: the cop rebounded from it and rubbed his neck, which had sustained the brunt of the impact. The second cop lunged and ricoshayed off Retief's other arm.

"What's the matter, you boys forgot how to open up a suitcase?" their leader inquired, producing a stout crowbar from a recess under the counter. "I'll show you," he added an instant before Retief plucked the iron bar from his grasp and carefully bent it into a rude circle, which he sent rolling across the cavernous shed floor. Both cops took a single step after it, and halted abruptly.

"You see what that Terry did?" one inquired of the circumambient air. "Took and twisted old Gluck's bar into a regler cookie," he amplified.

"He never," Gluck contradicted. "*Couldn't* of, Horace."

"I saw what I saw," Horace stated sullenly. "Leroy saw it too."

"I have a feeling you fellows been on this cushy indoor job too long," Gluck mused. "Thinking about transferring you out to foot-patrol on Big Rock." He glanced at Retief. "Big Rock's our near moon," he explained. "No air, no water, no snick berries. No much of anything. Keeps a fellow on his toes just trying to keep alive. Got a small Customs station out there.

"You wait here, Terry," he added in a harder tone, and set off toward a small partitioned-off room placed inconspicuously in a corner. He tapped diffidently at the door, over which Retief noted the words 'Liaison Office' and the equivalent in a variety of scipts, including the Ree ideograms. Gluck disappeared inside, and re-emerged a moment later accompanied by the squat, cylindrical figure of a Ree in military paint with the rank pips of a field grade officer. The alien outdistanced his escort to ripple truculently up to Retief.

"Gluck here—where the devil is the fellow?" the Ree interrupted himself to look around, discovering Gluck just behind him. "—says you got big ideas, Terry. Better shape up and show the boys your luggage, before I get tough."

"Keep a civil tongue in your talk-box," Retief ordered. "And you may address me as 'sir.' "

"Well," the colonel began hesitantly. "I've got my orders, Terry. It looks like I'll have to have you thrown in the lockup as a potential enemy alien."

"Potential?" Retief inquired. "Are you planning to start a war?"

"Well, you never know," the Ree declared. "Anyway, this is free Prutian soil, and I guess old Gluck's got a right to look through your laundry if he wants to."

"Are you and Gluck really sure you're ready to violate the most-favored-planet treaty between Terra and Prute?" Retief asked, as if mildly curious.

"Naw, nothing like that, Terry. Just routine, you know."

"Routine requires that diplomatic personnel in transit to friendly worlds be accorded duty-free entry of personal effects, and VIP treatment," Retief pointed out. "But, of course," he added, "we're willing to oil the routine."

He pulled out an envelope (funds, emergency, for good impression) and distributed a sheaf of

GUC. The Ree tentacled up the bulk, and the Purtians scooped the rest.

"You may stamp my passport now," Retief suggested, proferring the blue-covered booklet. "I'm in transit to Goldblatt's World, you know. Does that feeder flight originate here?"

"Suppose to," Gluck acknowledged, as he stamped a large purple impression on the blank transit visa page before him and handed the document back. "They'll make me sign a statement of charges for that pry-bar, you know," he added.

Retief allowed an extra five-Guck note to flutter down; Gluck plucked it from mid-air and whisked it out of sight.

"You know, Mister," he commented, "it's a real pleasure to be of service to a real gent like yourself, who knows where it's at. Lemme check on that cab." He hurried off toward the street doors.

4

When the porter had tossed Retief's trunk into the cargo bin of the dilapidated hack which had squealed to a halt at the inspector's imperious hail, and collected his half-Guck honorarium, the driver, a flabby-looking chap with a battered Bogan military-style peaked cap half-obscuring his face, leaned over the divider and said, "Where to, Mac?" in badly-accented Obfuscese.

"The Groaci Legation," Retief told him.

"You ain't no Groaci," the chauffer stated flatly. Retief agreed that the assessment was correct.

"Not enough eyes," the driver explained. "And no stems on the ones you got." He started up with a squeal of aged gyros and gunned the antique car into the traffic stream.

"Also, you're too high," he continued. "Look like one of them Terries, no offense."

"Flattered," Retief reassured his cicerone.

"I'm Jake. I've seen 'em all," the driver explained. "Wonder what a feller like you'd want with them Groaci. Hear old Snith throws anybody out on his can that comes around the place. Some nice guy, huh? Hope he ain't a friend o' yours."

"Not insofar as I know, Jake," Retief replied to the question. "I'm hoping he'll transmit a message to CIIU Slive for me."

"That sounds like one o' them Rees," Retief's new acquaintance stated. "No offense," he said, then added, "some folks say I shoot off my mouth too much. You a pal of them worms?" he queried, peering into his rear-view mirror at Retief.

"I haven't spent enough time with them to find out," Retief told him; "though they seem at their best when estivating in a sack."

The driver braked at a traffic square that opened suddenly between the tall, jut-front buildings at the end of the narrow street. Apparently they had come to a traffic roundabout, with individual initiative determining the cyclonic or anticyclonic flow.

The cab joined the majority of the movement, and changed course down another jut-front traffic slot. The driver took up his thoughts again and complained.

"You see them dang worms everywhere these

days. I got a feeling they're infiltrating, giving orders to honest Prutian folks right on their own planet. Heard they shot some folks who didn't get out of their way quick enough. We got no navy, you know."

"Sounds awkward," Retief commented. "What are you people doing about it?"

"Nothing," Jake said, "we got a mutual assistance pack with Terra, you know, and figger you boys'll swat these worms when the time is right. Right?"

"I hope so," Retief reassured Jake. "The problem is deciding when the time is right."

"Well, let's say sometime before they clean Prute out of all its food and fuel reserves," Jake suggested. "Say in about a week, the way they're going. They already cut my go-juice ration down to subsistence level, barely six glips a day. Feller'd starve on that, but lucky I got a few contacts."

"I'll make a note of it," Retief assured the anxious Prutian. "The short ration, I mean, not the contacts."

"There goes one of them worms now," Jake said, as the squat figure of a Ree enlisted trooper appeared ahead, hurrying across the crowded street, thrusting civilians aside as he went.

"Got a good mind to run the sucker down," Jake said, steering for the now isolated Ree, who had paused in mid-wriggle to light up a dope-stick.

"Better not," Retief suggested. "Wait for bigger game, like an Intimidator. Might as well get all the mileage you can, since it will be an interplanetary incident in either case."

Jake agreed and slowed; a moment later he swerved the cab sharply to pass between the baroquely ornamented columns flanking the gravelled drive of the Groacian Mission to Prute, jolting to a halt before the polished plastic plate with the words 'Legation of the Groacian Autonomy' and the fanciful armorial bearings of the Great Seal of Groac. Two uniformed Groaci Marines in smartly ribbed hip cloaks and silver-chased greaves snapped their eye-stalks and tentacles to attention as Retief disembarked from the wheezing vehicle and offered ten Guck to the driver, who grabbed the coin and gave the grimace of gratitude.

One of the guards lunged toward Retief, who put a finger under the Marine's third eye, the latter's momentum causing him to rebound, lose his balance, and fall heavily.

"You boys saw that," the Groaci yelled toward the driver and the other Marine. "Assault *and* battery, that's what it was! And maybe kidnapping, too, depending," he added, as his comrade helped him up.

"Don't worry," Retief counselled the Groaci. "If you don't accidentally blurt it out, nobody will ever know you tried it."

As the cab gunned away, the Marines closed ranks to bar Retief's entry.

"Who are you, Terry?" the aggressive one demanded.

"Special Terran Envoy Retief to see His Excellency," he informed the guards. "He's expecting me."

"To doubt that His Excellency has time for distressed Terry tourists," one guard offered, as the other vibrated his throat-sac in the Groaci equivalent of a snicker.

"No doubt," Retief agreed. "But I'm not a sightseer." He brushed the nearer guard aside and, as the second Marine came to port arms, standing his ground, Retief plucked the weapon from his grasp and snapped the breech open. He glanced down the pitted barrel and tossed the blaster back to its owner.

"You forgot to clean that piece this year, Lance Corporal," he told the indignant Groaci. "Fire the thing in that condition and it's likely to blow your head off. Now let's see you get that door open."

The chastened guard, his crest adroop, moved quickly to comply with Retief's order. His partner erected all five eye-stalks in an expression of Ferocity Restrained (Z-21) and resumed his place at one side of the door. Retief passed between the two alert sentries into the gloomy, smoked gribble-grub smell of the Groaci Mission. A pert receptionist at a small desk looked up brightly.

"To inquire your business," she said as sharply as her weak Groaci voice would permit.

"Just want to see his nibs, sweetheart," Retief told her.

"The Consul is receiving no callers without a proper appointment," she returned sharply.

"That's good," Retief replied calmly, "because I've got one that was made by Undersecretary Snaffle personally. Via closed screen, that is."

"Oh." The young Groaci female said contritely. "You'd think the old sourpuss would tip me off." She checked a small computer terminal, came up with a print-out card which she handed over.

"The Chancery is one floor up, to the left; second door on your left. I'm supposed to tell you not to snoop. But I'm sure you're too nice for that, anyway."

"I'm sure His Ex will tell me all I need to know, with no necessity for snooping,' Retief reassured her.

The lift was an antique Otis, formerly installed in Macy's, Retief noted, from the ornate wrought-iron monogram worked into the cage ceiling. It wheezed and clanked its way upward like an exhausted alpinist making the last few yards to the survival hut. When precisely between floors, it came to an abrupt halt.

Retief pushed the appropriate buttons. They elicited no response. He stood still and listened. He heard a distant thumping and the faint sound of shouting. The words were impossible to distinguish, but the intonation was definitely Terran. Retief pushed open the escape hatch on the ceiling of the car, and pulled himself up and out on the six-foot-square roof. The thumping and yelling were louder here. Above, he saw a small hinged panel set in the wall of the elevator shaft. He was able to reach it by climbing the greasy cable which supported the elevator car. A sharp kick against the latch mechanism caused the panel to pop open. Now the thumping and shouts sounded clearly.

". . . let us *out*! Let us out!", the shout was repeated, in frontier Terran. The pounding went on monotonously. Looking into the cramped crawl-space the panel had covered, Retief saw light leaking from somewhere at the far end of the passage. He worked his way in, and proceeded on elbows and toes, through dust and arachnid-webs, complete with arachnids, until he reached a crudely boarded-over opening in the side wall, through which the light was leaking.

"Let us *out*!" the chant went on, accompanied by thumps. "Let us *out*! Ah, hell, Andy, what's the use? Nobody can hear us, and even if they did, who's around to give a hang what happens to a bunch of Terry POW's?"

Retief got a fingertip grip on a plank and ripped it free. Now he could see into a featureless gray cell, lit by a ragged hole in one wall through which wan Prutian sunlight streamed. Half a dozen assorted Terrans—men, women and one thumb-sucking five-year old—sat in dejected attitudes on the littered floor. All looked up as one at the *scritch*! of the torn-away plank. The child eyed him solemnly for a moment, then removed his thumb from his mouth, wiped it carefully on his grubby chemise, and uttered a wail. His mother caught him up, casting a reproachful glance toward Retief.

"Holy Moses," a youngish fellow in faded bib overalls said and came to his feet. "Who're you, feller? And how'd you get in the cross-shaft system?"

"The elevator stopped and I heard you yelling," Retief told him. "I get the idea you'd rather be elsewhere."

"Too right," a small man with a villainous two-weeks' growth of black whiskers volunteered.

An elderly man wearing a once-elegant but now badly torn and stained suit got creakily to his feet.

"We're hostages," the latter said. "Seems the Ree big shot, this fellow who calls himself Slive, has an idea we're worth money, or at least territorial concessions. Damn fool. What does the CDT care what happens to us?"

"Actually," Retief told him, "We'd heard something about you folks: that's why I'm here, in a way. Are you all the hostages they have?"

"You could have plumb swaggled me," the oldster conceded. "I reckoned we were good for a life stretch. I'm Governor Anderson of Peabody's Plantation, out on Hardtack. Was, anyway, until those confounded Rees landed one morning whilst I was on my south forty, and rounded up what folks they could find.

"This," he added, indicating the small be-whiskered man, "is my boy Lester, and his wife, Lulu, and little Roy. Other feller's Buster, my hired hand. There's more, from some other settlement, I guess. Just got a glimpse of them whilst we was unloading. About two dozen altogether, I reckon. Who're you? How come you're in that cross-shaft? They boarded it over the first day we was here, about a month ago, or maybe a week . . ." The old fellow paused to study a pattern of scratches on the nacreous wall beside him. "Yep, thirty-two days today."

Retief tossed aside two more of the slats barring his egress, and dropped down into the cramped and smelly room. The furnishings, he noted, consisted of two battered mattresses laid on the floor, half a dozen pots, some rugs of dubious origin and a scattering of papers, one of which, face-up, read AN INVITATION TO ALL SQUATTERS TO ACCEPT LIBERATION BY VICTORIOUS REE ARMIES. THIS MEANS YOU.

"I take it you'd like to get out of here," Retief said to the ex-governor.

"Oh, it ain't so bad," Buster, the hired hand, contributed, "only no telly."

"Lord yes, sir," daughter-in-law Lulu put in fervently. "Roy needs better eats and more of 'em. Can't hardly yell good a-tall."

"What you got in mind, Mister?" son Lester demanded eagerly, coming to his feet. He was clad in a grayish sack-like garment. His exposed hide, dark with lack of bathing facilities, was marked with angry red flea-bites, at which he scratched absently, awaiting a reply.

"For the moment," Retief told him, "just sit tight and stay alert. Break off the banging and chanting, but the next time they feed you, eat all you can, because you may be missing a few meals."

"Won't mind that," the hired hand said. "They feed worserner'n the Navy: I was in fer a couple weeks," he amplified. "Reserves. But they told us they run outa funds, whatever funds are, and they up and disbanded us. Too bad, too, jest a month afore the Rees showed up. We were expecting a couple Terry battlewagons would come along and run the worms off, but they never."

"Back at GHQ," Retief said, "the top officials aren't really sure there's a war on, so they've been a bit slow to respond. Maybe we can speed things up a little."

"Whatever you say, Mister," Lester blurted. "But we can't do much a-setting here."

"True," Retief conceded. "Just be ready to go. Don't try to follow me; that duct is a dead end. And remember: try not to start any riots."

5

Retief retraced his route to the elevator, this time operating the emergency switch on top of the car, and resumed his slow progress upward. At last the rickety cage clanked to a halt, meticulously leveled itself, and the doors *whoosh*!ed open. Retief stepped out into a corridor garishly carpeted in chartreuse and puce and went along to a forbidding set of double doors at the end of the passage. A cocoa mat lettered STAY AWAY lay before them.

Retief tapped lightly and heard a breathy reply from inside. He tried the door; locked. He twisted harder and something broke with a sharp *tink*! and the door swung in. Across the wide room, a Groaci wearing the jeweled eye-shields of a top-three-grader glanced at him.

"To explain the meaning of this outrage!" he hissed.

"It means that Terry diplomats with appointments aren't cooling their heels in the corridor this year, Mr. Consul," Retief interpreted. "I need to see the Ree Intimidator Slive, and I'm informed you're prepared to offer your good offices in arranging the meeting."

Consul Snith canted three eyestalks at an angle indicative of gracious condescension and rose to his full four-foot-eight. "To have no time to devote to such trifles," he hissed, after a brief glance at the embossed card Retief had handed him. "Only a Second Secretary and Consul, eh?" he whispered, "Not even a Counsellor."

"True, Mr. Consul," Retief acknowledged. "Still I *would* have been a Counsellor, if anybody had gotten around to promoting me."

"Of course," Snith agreed. "And at the same time, I myself would now be an Undersecretary by the same reasoning, thus maintaining the disparity in rank. But enough of this yivshish. I suppose I can deal with you, just this once. After all, all I'm going to do is refuse to help you."

"Since your Mission has the only hot-line to Ree HQ in the Tip," Retief countered, "it wouldn't take a moment to get through to the Intimidator."

"But that I refuse to do," Snith hissed.

"So I guess I'll have to do it myself," Retief replied, coming around the twelve-foot platinum desk, Chief of Mission, for the use of.

The Groaci lunged for a drawer in time to encounter Retief's hand, which closed on his skinny tentacle and lifted him from his Terry-made hip-o-matic power swivel chair, a gift of Ambassador Fullthrust on the occasion of the signing of the latest in a series of treaties of Eternal Chumship, none of which had been effective in diminishing the traditional rivalry between the Galactic super-powers.

Snith delivered a breathy tirade in which the repetitive "vile Terry" and "iniquitious Soft One" soon became tiresome.

Retief dropped the senior diplomat into his own solid gold wastebasket, abruptly ending the stream of threats of dire retribution.

The traditional red-enameled tight-beam personal screen built into the desk uttered a harsh buzz when Retief flipped the URGENT key.

At once, an unctious voice said, in flawless Groaci: "To wait whilst one notifies the Second Assistant Great One to notify the First AGO to intimate to the Great One himself that some lesser being is understandably desirous of holding converse with his Loftiness."

"To put some snap into it," Retief replied in Groaci over the tight-beam, without heat.

Snith redoubled his threshing among the waste paper and keened: "To walk softly, Retief! To not arouse the ire of the insidious Ree against selfless Groacian bureaucrats!"

"Don't worry, Mr. Consul," Retief soothed his host. "I'm only talking to the janitor."

"To have heard that crack," the hot line said harshly. "Maybe you five-eyed suckers don't know us building supers got a union, which we could shut down custodial services to you boys any time. Your wastebasket would get pretty full, if the sweeper corps didn't show up at dark to rub old Pennzoil on the desk-tops to give 'em that nice shine, which you old-timers know enough not to put your elbows onna desk till about after lunch."

"A telling point!" Snith hissed from his cramped position in the disposal bin. "To apologize at once, Retief, lest this miscreant implement his threat!"

"To be in a slight hurry," Retief said into the talker in unaccented Groaci, "To have to talk to Slive right now."

There was a crackle of static from the beam, an echo of secretarial huffings, and a new voice cut in, speaking Groaci with a heavy Ree accent.

"This is His Loftiness speaking. "What've you got, Snith? I was just revising my surprise—ha-ha—plans for receiving a delegation of Terries."

"To rejoice in the intelligence, Loftiness," Retief

returned, mimicking Groaci eagerness. "To yearn to revel in the details."

"Sure, why not?" Slive replied comfortably. "You little five-eyed sticky-fingers are just as neutral against the Terries as us Ree. So here's the plot: We got a couple dozen Terry hostages; you know, like the ones you're keeping for me," Slive continued, "picked 'em up pretending they were simple farmers and colonists out on some end-of-the-line worlds they call Moosejaw, and Hardtack and a couple others. Since they weren't in uniform, we've got a right to shoot 'em as spies, of course."

"To be sure," Retief agreed. "What did they spy on?"

"Well, of course us Ree've got nothing to hide," Slive replied. "But still some of them might've got a glimpse of some of the peaceful missile installations we've been installing on a few small bodies in monitored space and all. Could get talk started, as if us Ree would do anything as lousy as infiltrating inviolate Treaty Territory."

"Small minds *do* tend to misinterpret these matters," Retief agreed cheerfully. "Anything else?"

"They could've got an idea there's something fishy about our new out-tourist program," Slive conceded. "We've been encouraging solid Ree citizens with impeccable security records to get culturally enriched by traveling around in what the Terries call Tip Space, learning all about the quaint native arts of basket-weaving and electronic surveillance, and early-warning sites, and folk-dancing—all that culture stuff, you know."

"Good thinking, Intimidator," Retief replied

crisply. "To tell me more about the doubtless clever surprise you have in store for the delegation of vile Terry meddlers you're expecting."

"Well, this is pretty good, Snith, old boy," Slive replied. "I've got a couple schemes, but I about decided on just a simple defenestration. My offices are on the ninety-third floor, you know."

"To first disarm them if they should so far violate diplomatic usage as to attempt to smuggle weapons into the conference room, of course," Retief guessed. "Then to extort humiliating terms of peace, and once signatures are in hand, to dispose of them. Superb!"

"You get the sketch," Slive agreed. "But this is top security dope. My Chief of Security'll go into a premature moult if he knew I was talking about it, even on this tight line to my pal Snith."

"To assure you, it will go no further," Retief assured the Ree warlord. "Now, about that delegation: I myself have assumed the responsibility of requesting your reception of such a party, at your convenience, on the third day of the Moon of Impeccable Treachery, a salubrious season for your clever plan, eh?"

"Suits me, Snith. Make it between one-thirty and six pee em. Better have the old credentials in order, too."

"To assume lunch will be served in the waiting room," Retief suggested.

"They'll have to wait in the baggage shed, which has a gribble-grub dispenser and a Pepsi machine," Slive replied harshly. "Why waste VIP eats on alimentary tracts that won't be around long enough to digest 'em?"

"Splendid," Retief said in Snith's breathiest, most enthusiastic tone. "Since the gribble-grub

dispensers were a gift of the Groacian people to
Ree, to enjoy a sense of participation in the
scheme."

"Don't go grabbing the credit, Mr. Consul,"
Slive came back sharply. "After all, you boys
are Easterners, too, like the Terries, and to tell
you the truth, I don't see why you'd want to
lend us West Arm fellows a hand to take over
your own turf."

"To pretend not to have heard that, Slive,"
Retief replied stiffly. "An opportunity to wipe
the eye of the vile Terries is at any cost not to be
allowed to pass me by."

"Just don't get any ideas you're getting cut in
for a slice of the action," Slive warned. "I agreed
to tolerate you boys and give you preferential
status when it come to doling out menial jobs,
is all."

"The litter-mate of nest-fouling drones is too
arrogant by half!" Snith hissed from his position in the waste receptacle. "To perhaps reconsider my rash agreement to aid him in his
aggressive designs."

"I heard that, Snith," Slive yelled. "Stand a
little closer, I almost lost you on that last
transmission. Reconsider, eh? Better get your
fleet out of mothballs!"

"On that note, Mr. Consul," Retief said to the
excited Groaci, "I shall take my leave. Ta."

6

Leaving the Groaci Legation, Retief found his
taxi awaiting him.

"I figgered in case you came out of there alive,
you wouldn't be in no condition for no long
walk," Jake confided.

"Take me to the best hotel in town," Retief specified, to the amusement of his chauffer.

"That'd be the Prutian Hilton," Jake offered when his hilarity had subsided. "Funny," he added, "a hotel can be the best without being good."

After half an hour's limping progress through crowded streets in which a shabby elegance steadily deteriorated, the vehicle wheezed to a stop before a peeling polystyrene facade ornamented with new neon letters six feet high, in the crabbed Prutian script, identifying it as an outpost of Hilton enterprise.

Inside, Retief found his way along a corridor which was either still under construction or in the final stages of collapse—he was unable to determine which—up rickety stairs to a door painted a dull turnbuckle dun, adorned with a yellow 6, and hanging by one hinge. The interior of the chamber fulfilled the rich promise of its context. An almost-clean spot on the lone, tarnished window afforded a view of the street, where a squat, black-enameled vehicle parked before the hotel was disgorging three Prutian Cops who hurried inside in a purposeful manner.

Retief returned to the narrow hall, took up a position behind heaped crates at the head of the stairs. As the first of the local cops arrived, puffing, Retief stepped out suddenly, causing the squat Prutian to shy violently; Retief saved him from a painful tumble back down the steps by a quick grab.

"Hi, there," Retief said casually. "Good of you to come. What I wanted was directions to the VIP entrance to the Port Departures area."

"Thanks, pal," the cop muttered, readjusting his tunic, by the collar of which Retief had hauled him to safety. "You want to find the VIP gate, what you do, you go right past the public entry, that's figgering you're coming up along Condemned Parkway, and hang a right. Straight past the baggage-smashing department, over the NO PASSAGE BEYOND THIS POINT barrier, or maybe through it, if you're driving a heavy vehicle, and through the door marked Prutian Ladies Only, and there you are. You'll never find it. Come on, the boys and I'll run you over."

Retief ambled downstairs after his guide.

Back in the street, the lieutenant greeted his minions, "Yeah, this is the Terry Retief we were supposed to pick up. But I don't lean over backwards to pick guys up for the Groaci, and this one gave me a hand when the grand stairway collapsed. Saved my life, maybe. He's in a hurry, got to catch Ten Planet Flight 79 at three o'clock. Let's rush him there—and we've no time to waste."

Chapter Three

Accompanied by his escort, Retief arrived at the Ten Planet check-in station at 2:59, to be greeted wanly by a string-thin Prutian who glanced a Retief's ticket, supplied by the Transport Officer at Sector some days earlier, and said off-handedly:

"Must be some foul-up, Terry. You've got no reservation. Wouldn't have mattered if you had, actually. Flight 79 lifted ten minutes ago." The clerk patted back a yawn and looked past Retief, who commented mildly, "Jumped the gun, didn't it?"

"You don't have to get *nasty*!" the counterman protested, his pinched face pale with rage. "How else do you think T-P can maintain its rep for punctual arrivals? Besides, you were actually booked on the *Irresponsible*, which was lost in space a week ago. Probably shot up by the Ree. They pretend they're palsy-walsy, but I don't trust the dastards," the travel agent elaborated.

"I put you on stand-by for 79, which you missed. Hardly *my* fault."

"Anything else going that way?" Retief asked.

"Certainly *not!*" was the reply. "No one with good sense would want to go out to any of those frontier hell-holes with all these Ree infiltrating, anyway."

"Right," Retief said firmly. As he turned away, an elderly Yill bystander with the appearance of a soup-kitchen regular put out a scrawny gray hand and said in a ratchety voice:

"Hold hard, Terry. Happens my vessel is bound for Tip space. Might be able to help you out, if you've got no objection to riding with a cargo of glimp eggs which I admit I held a bit too long, waiting for the market to go up."

"Thanks, Captain," Retief replied. "When are we lifting?"

"Well," the old spacedog replied, "See, I've got this bad leg, so if you want to take the load in for me, I'll see you get ten percent, plus of course it's a free ride. I'll need about a hundred Guck for port fees."

Retief handed over a hundred-Guck note and accompanied his new acquaintance, Captain M'hu hu by name, to the transport bar, where the old fellow downed a dozen stiff shots of Hellrose before Retief had finished his Bacchus black.

"Feller'd hafta be crazy to go out there in these here parlous times," the captain commented. His bleary gaze fell on Retief. "Figger to get me drunk and con me into letting you ride along without no visa, eh, Terry? Well, you picked the wrong pigeon; 'Cap M'hu hu can hold his booze' is a saying that's knowed from

Azoll to Zoob: So you can just dust off, Terry, after you buy me one more."

Retief took the old fellow by his bony elbow, led him out along a service passage to the glass wall fronting the wind-swept ramp where space-scarred hulls in fantastic variety stood festooned with service cables. Captain M'hu hu pointed out one of the shabbiest, parked well down the line, as his own command, *Cockroach III*.

"Fine a little embargo-buster as ever run a load of Feeb seed into Groac, and the five-eyed little beggars are allergic to it," he stated proudly.

Retief requested and received, not without protest, the undocking codes and master electro-key, the captain grumpily accepting a second hundred-Guck note in return.

"Place she's programmed for they call Goblin-rock; you hear a lotta superstitions about the place. Actually, it's jest about deserted; watch out for some big gray cactus things, is all. You'll get there OK, maybe," M'hu hu guessed, "but getting back out's somethin else. So long, sucker."

Retief bade M'hu hu farewell, but as he started through the door leading outside, the old fellow set up an outcry like a gut-shot dire-beast, yelling that he hadn't been paid. Retief up-ended the noisy old grifter in a handy public convenience, and boarded the ancient vessel without further complications. After a few minutes devoted to scanning the operating manual, he used the electrokey, and lifted off.

2

The rattles, buzzes, clatters, knocks, thumps and wails of the old tub, Retief soon noticed, were more noisy than threatening. The thousand-tonner lifted smoothly; the autopilot, already programmed, maneuvered the craft through the intricate departure pattern and took up course, Retief noted, in the general direction of Goldblatt's remote world.

Days passed without incident, other than a half-hearted pass by a Ree torpedo boat whose peremptory hail Retief ignored. A few hours later, a heavy gunboat bearing the Ree blazon closed course with the tramp freighter and hailed:

"All right, M'hu hu, don't get any big ideas. What's the idea trying to cut the boys on the PT out of the action?"

"The fun's over, fellows," Retief replied. "Captain M'hu hu has retired, and the run has been taken over by the Terran Space Arm. Better clear space to port, because this is where I try out my new evaporator beams. I wouldn't want to vaporize you by accident."

The gunboat, which had fallen in alongside at ten miles, edged away and fell slightly astern. Meanwhile, red alarm lights had flashed on all across the freighter's board. On the forward screen, a meteorite-pocked body of irregular shape had come into view dead ahead.

"Now, Terry," the Ree vessel resumed transmission, "I don't know what you've got in mind, but I guess you know enough to sheer off and give Goblinrock a wide berth."

The gunboat fired a shot in parting, and fell farther astern. At the same time, the freighter's innards began to groan, and the big DISASTER IMMINENT light glared angrily. Retief made adjustments to the autopilot to steer directly for the rock ahead.

The gunboat had backed off to fifty miles without further comment or gunfire. Retief's forward screens showed the pinkish orb of the barren moon at extreme range but coming up fast. A few moments later, the first tentative *thump*!s of atmosphere contact shook the elderly vessel, setting off the master alarm systems which shrilled and *bang*!ed and flashed red letters reading ALL SYSTEMS IN FAILURE MODE.

Retief rode the disintegrating hulk down to ten thousand feet before ejecting. The escape pod's air system was inoperative, he noted, but a quick resetting of valves expelled the foul air and allowed the fresh, thin air of Goblinrock to fill the cramped space only moments before the pod's landing jacks made violent contact with the satellite's surface.

The pod wobbled, but stabilized at last. Retief forced the hatch open and emerged into breathlessly hot, but breathable air. He found himself in a hard-baked desert of dun and ochre mud reticulated by heat-cracks.

A barely visible trail of vapor marked the path his stricken craft had followed in its meteoric descent. The point of contact was clearly indicated by a column of denser smoke.

Nearby was a patch of spiny growths resembling pink Christmas trees. Retief stood in the sparse shade of the 'trees' and scanned the hazy pink horizon, dead flat except for an occasional upthrust spine of unweathered rock.

Retief examined the fleshy leaves of the nearest tree, noting that its glossy, leather-like surface was distinctly cool to the touch. As he fingered the leaf, it seemed to quiver, then to twitch away from his touch. He tried another, with the same result. Then he noticed that the other plants appeared to be more closely clustered about him than they had been a moment before. He stepped back, jostling a small tree close behind him. As he side-stepped it, he was quite sure that it somehow leaned into his path, pressing against him more insistently as he thrust harder against it.

"Let's be reasonable, Pushy," Retief said aloud. "You stand still and I'll get out of your way."

At his next step, the tree to the right seemed to shift position to close off the gap through which he had been about to step clear of the thicket. Retief set his feet, grasped the nearest branch, which felt like a fleshy overlay on a hard core, bent it back until a thin wail sounded from some indefinable point amid the foliage. Holding the branch aside, he advanced a step, and paused again to push aside two more stout limbs which he had not previously noticed, barring his way.

After a moment's consideration, Retief turned and tried another direction, found it as densely obstructed, as was every side. Now he felt a touch at his shoulder, and a moment later the questing shoot which had brushed him whipped around his neck, constricting.

"Naughty," Retief said mildly as he forced his thumb under the pencil-thick tendril and pried it away, unwound it, and tied it in a square-knot. At once, the flexible growth went limp. Meanwhile, another strand had encircled his upper arm and another his ankle, to be dealt with in the same way. Retief paused; the heat was apalling.

"No fair, O Motile One," a telepathically communicated voice said, without audible sound.

"You introduce intolerable complexities into what should have been a simple and much-needed ingestional process."

"That's the way we motile ones are," Retief responded. He took a knife from the survival kit attached to his belt and tested the edge with his thumb. "I suggest you boys keep your branches to yourselves," he added, "so that it won't be necessary for me to demonstrate the principle of the cutting edge."

"You threaten the Surviving One?" the mind-voice queried coldly. "Perhaps it will be as well if we proceed at once to pre-digestion. Very well, fellows, melt it down."

At once a fine spray of cool moisture enveloped the Terran. The fluid appeared to be expelled in minute droplets from pores covering the surface of leaves and stems alike. A drop trickled down Retief's upper lip, as the voice spoke again:

"You, O formerly Motile One, are now enveloped in a cloud of the most corrosive substance in nature. Prepare to be dissolved."

"That wouldn't be H_2O, I suppose," Retief hazarded as his tongue touched the droplet on his lip.

"Precisely. Our methods of preparing nourishment are unparalleled. We ourselves are of course impervious to this caustic compound."

"I dare you to step up the volume," Retief said.

The swiftly evaporating mist had lowered the temperature to a bearable level, and his heat-parched skin was eagerly absorbing the water, which was now trickling down in an increased volume.

"You presume, O Motile One, to attempt to resist the corrosive action of the universe's most potent solvent?"

"Sure," Retief said. "I don't have time to be dissolved right now. If you boys are hungry, I'm in a position to offer you a full cargo of gourmet delights, if it isn't splashed all over the landscape, that is; or even if it is. I don't suppose you'd object to having to collect it."

"It is well known to us, impertinent one, that all edible matter on this our world has long since been consumed. We ourselves discovered and ingested the last patch of nourishing lichen some centuries agone."

"Good news:" Retief told the silent voice. "It's lunchtime. The only problem is that we're here, and lunch is a couple of miles away. By the way, you can call me Retief."

"Yes," Pushy agreed. "We are but now examining the phenomenon, Retief, and the aroma of roasting protein is indeed most appetizing; we seem to recall having sampled something similar, and arranging for a resupply with the obliging mariner M'hu hu. We are of course not ungrateful to you, Retief, for descending from emptiness to bring this gift. You may therefore crave a boon of us."

"Well, boonwise," Retief answered. "Let's start by giving up the idea of eating me. Then we can work on the details."

"When you approached within our reflexive radius," Pushy replied, registering surprise, "we assumed you were volunteering your person as an *aperetif*. Such an act of self-immolation evoked our deepest gratitude. Pity you spoiled it by failing to dissolve."

"Thoughtless of me," Retief agreed. "Now, if you'll stop trying to fence me off, I'll check the pod and see if its ground maneuvering gear is operable."

At once there was a stir, and a clear avenue appeared through the thick-clustered growths, which now surrounded Retief in depth in all directions. He walked out along the open lane into the blinding sunlight, much refreshed by his soaking, the continuing evaporation of which served admirably to absorb the circumambient heat which otherwise would have hard-boiled a man in three minutes.

He went back to the pod, which was perched awkwardly but intact on its sprung jacks. He climbed in, and was pleased to find that the SURFACE GEAR—DE-PLOY lever elicited a laborious but effective response, bringing the pod to a level attitude. A light indicated TRACKS UNDER LOAD. The power-pack was at half charge; on command, the capsule moved off jerkily in the correct direction. The steering was stiff, but accurate, and after half an hour of bumpy progress, Retief arrived at the smouldering heap of glue rubbish that had been *Cockroach III*.

He climbed out into the smoky stink of incinerated glimp eggs to find the stand of pink organisms clustered close beside him.

"I see you're pretty motile yourself, Pushy," Retief commented mentally.

"We decline to expend our waning energies in feckless perambulations," the silent voice said. "We long ago made the decision to adopt the plant kingdom's strategy of immobility, except, of course, in the event of emergency. The present occasion so qualifies. It occurs to us," Pushy went on, "that your mode of arrival, or that of your cargo carrier, could be improved upon, maintenance-of-equipment-wise."

"I was having a little emergency of my own," Retief explained. "She started coming apart when I hit atmosphere—thin as it was."

"Perhaps, after we have gleaned the nourishment from the debris, you would like us to reassemble the craft, the design of which, though primitive, seems serviceable enough."

"Go right ahead, fellows," Retief agreed. "But be careful with the power core; it could be leaky."

"We had noted a high flux-density of rather short wavelength emanating from the larger fragment—there," Pushy replied, extending a finger-like tendril to point to what remained of the drive unit of *Cockroach III*.

"I see you fellows are ahead of me," Retief acknowledged. "By the way, is it 'fellows,' or just 'fellow'? Are you a crowd, or just one individual?"

"We are many-in-one," Pushy replied. "Of the teeming species that formerly peopled this once-fair world I alone remain. We determined early in our evolution that the linkage of the many relatively feeble organisms to comprise one potent being, thus ending the inter-being and inter-species rivalry, would enhance our ability to survive under increasingly hostile conditions, as our atmosphere and hydrosphere dissipated into space, and our surface minerals were removed by the Ree banditti."

"That sounds like a neat trick," Retief conceded. "But how do you manage without food and water?"

"From time to time we receive a gift of organic matter from He Who is Powerful, recently usually in the form of these same objectionable creatures who call themselves 'Ree,' and who come here—or formerly did—to replenish their stores of various minerals. When we approached them, in innocent curiosity, they turned weapons upon us, from the destructive effects of which we are only now recovering. Candidly, when you came to rest and emerged from your chrysalis, we assumed at first that you, too, were of the odious Ree, and would attempt to help yourself to the substance of this our world. When we saw that you offered us no harm, we realized our error, and would have incorporated your ego-gestalt into our own. But you dissuaded us, by your curious immunity to dissolution in water, which dissolves all substances."

"You seem to have done an excellent job of surviving," Retief said.

By now, the pink conoids had encircled the smoking wreck and were busily extending pseudopodia to gather in the well-cooked masses of glimp egg. They were well along with the task when, abruptly, Pushy spoke again.

"Retief, we note that a vessel of the insidious Ree is approaching, on a vector which will bring it to rest at this precise point in fourteen minutes and three seconds from . . . now."

"Thanks for the warning," Retief replied. "Do you have any ideas?"

"We shall cope with the intruder in our usual fashion," Pushy replied coolly. "We suggest that you re-enter your husk and withdraw to ten miles until we have restored tranquility."

"I'll pull back a little way and keep an eye on the action," Retief said. "Just in case this fellow has a new trick or two up his sleeve. Good luck."

With that Retief climbed back into the pod, and trundled it off over the heat-baked plain to a point of vantage atop a rocky ridge. Adjusting his DV scanner for maximum gain, he watched as the tree-like pink organism disposed itself in a loose ring around the crash site.

Moments later, the gunboat which had earlier fired on *Cockroach III* executed a neat landing beside the blackened wreckage. At once, in accordance with SOP, it fired the usual anti-personnel charges; the shrapnel *whoof*!ed into the fleshy pink growths, sending gouts of Pushy's substance spattering.

The ring closed in slightly but showed no other response. A hatch near the prow of the blunt Ree fleetboat opened, and half a dozen squat Ree made their way to ground, well ensconced in protective suits. They approached the wreckage cautiously.

Retief tuned the pod's pickup to the Ree wavelength; the filters clarified the creaky reception until he overheard:

"—no doubt the goblins got him, the damned fool."

"Escape pod's gone, Sergeant. Maybe . . ."

"Never mind the maybes. Just check until you find the remains. And look out for tall yellow cactuses."

The Ree troopers climbed over the cooling wreckage, poking and rummaging.

"Not here, Sergeant," someone said. "Probably

burnt up, if the goblins din't get him, like you said."

"All I said was 'probably,' soldier!" the non-commissioned officer in charge corrected. "Keep looking."

After half an hour of this fruitless endeavor, the Ree returned to the scant shade under the stern of their vessel, formed up in a column of twos, unlimbered heat weapons, and deployed within the gradually closing ring of pink trees.

Retief at once maneuvered the pod in the shelter of the ridge to the point closest to the wreck, then emerged at full speed and drove directly toward the Ree gunboat, parked only a few yards beyond the remains of *Cockroach III*.

The Ree troops broke formation and sprinted for their boat, all but two who Retief saw were ensnared by outreaching tendrils of Pushy-stuff.

He came careening in a cloud of dust, skidded between wreck and boat, sending the last of the Ree who had been waiting to board flying for shelter behind whatever rocks they could find. Only then did a few random shots ricochet harmlessly from the pod's hull.

"We express our thanks, Retief," Pushy's insubstantial voice came clearly to Retief. "In another moment, the noxious invaders might have done us a mischief. Though we find the substance of those few we harvested most refreshing."

It seemed to Retief that the voice strengthened even as it spoke. He halted and brought the pod around in a curve to rest beside the clustered pink growth, from which cables now extended to the gunboat, probing around its closed hatches.

"Alas," the mind-voice came again. "We find

this material proof against our solvents and our strength alike."

"Wait a minute," Retief suggested. "Maybe I can open that sardine can for you."

As he stepped down from the pod, he saw the boat's aft battery rotate jerkily and come to rest aimed dead at the pod. He hurried over to the main entry hatch, which, as he had expected, had been retrofitted with an economy-model Bogan electrolock. A quick and simple adjustment to the key to *Cockroach III* adapted it to fit—and the hatch cycled open.

At once, a wrist-thick pink rootlet jostled him and started inside the airlock. Retief caught it, wrenched the tough member to one side, where it felt its way blindly along the undercurve of the Ree hull.

"I'd almost forgotten why I call you 'Pushy,' Pushy," Retief told the organism, which was now, he observed, in the process of modifying its external form to that of a cluster of pale blue puff-balls, their feathery spines waving gently, like underwater fronds.

The member which had attempted to enter the airlock was now returning as a wiry, dark-blue filament. Retief caught it and tied it to a stanchion in a loose slip-knot.

"That substance change is a neat trick, Pushy," Retief commented. "No wonder the Ree started believing in goblins."

"Why do you seek to spoil our sport, Retief?" the voice said sulkily. "Once you rendered valuable assistance, yet now you seek to obstruct our just vengeance."

"You've had a good meal," Retief pointed out.

"You don't need this snack. Let's negotiate, instead."

"To what end?" Pushy demanded. "Release my probe at once, and there'll be an end to these scoundrels!"

"There'll just be more scoundrels coming along to even the score," Retief pointed out. "These fellows are taking over the Arm, or they will if I let them. This is a good opportunity to correct their thinking."

"Very well," Pushy acceded reluctantly. "But I was envisioning the pleasure of ingesting their nutrients, slowly."

"I'll make it a part of the deal that they keep you supplied with glimp eggs," Retief offered. "I'm pretty sure they'll be in a mood to deal generously."

With that, he entered the dim-lit, kippered herring smelling air-lock and used the standard-model talker to demand audience with the captain, who identified himself as Bliff. He informed the officer that he had come to offer a possibility of survival.

"I'll blow you off the face of this Blurb-forsaken rock!" Captain Bliff replied heatedly.

"Don't," Retief cautioned. "It would spoil this nice beginning. Now let's talk terms."

"You wish to surrender?" Bliff queried hopefully.

"Don't let's waste time with jokes," Retief replied sternly. "If you'll lift off, report to HQ that Goblinrock is worse than ever, and arrange for a monthly shipment of glimp eggs and otherwise stay 10 A.U.'s away, I'll do what I can to see that you're not dissolved in digestive juices at your post."

"Sounds horrible," Bliff commented. "At my post, you say? Strange, these goblins—masters of disguise—I was told they were long, skinny purple fellows, and my non-coms swore they were prickly yellow things. Seems we were both wrong."

"That, Captain, is the understatement of the year," Retief told him.

3

"I suggest you accept, Pushy," Retief advised the compound being upon his return from inside the Ree boat. "It's the best deal you'll get. Captain Bliff was forced to land here because of a breakdown in his converter circuits. He landed beside the wreck because it was the only sign of life he saw. He was on the lookout for big yellow sausages, which it seems is the shape you were using the last time a Ree got away from here alive."

"I recall," the blue puffballs replied. "We were so busy mopping up the tasty morsels packed into the hold—it was a troopship— that we failed to notice one unit making a sneaky getaway in a lifeboat. Pity."

"Maybe not," Retief demurred. "The loss of a fully loaded troop carrier made an impression on Ree HQ. They put Goblinrock off limits. But now, by repairing this gunboat and sending it off safe and sound, you'll have a steady supply of food and no more harassment."

"I concede the proposal has its advantages," Pushy concurred. "I suppose we may as well contain ourselves in patience until the first load of goodies arrives—and after that, perhaps we'll reconsider."

"Don't," Retief advised firmly. "They can stand off and bombard you from space easily enough, but if you're providing a repair and refit station, they'll hold off."

"Very well," the puffball agreed. "Just get that hatch open again and we'll set things to rights in there."

Retief opened the hatch an inch, and the blue tendril entered after a final caution from Retief not to snack between meals, to reemerge half a minute later.

"Simple enough," the silent voice reported. "Merely a matter of matching resultance in the boomer circuits." At that moment, the mended gunboat emitted a soft buzzing and lifted off, reoriented itself and sped away.

"OK," the now-blue organism said, with a crisp change of subject, "perhaps we'd best see to the reconstruction of your own somewhat cryptic vessel. Tell me, Retief, is it correct for its components to be deployed over three quarters of an acre, or was it formerly more tightly organized?"

"It was all in one piece," Retief explained. "Except for a certain amount of wear and tear."

"We shall examine the components, and deduce their original configuration as best we can," Pushy said briskly.

Retief watched as the blue entity sent out a multitude of wiry shoots to quest over the wreckage, apparently unaffected by the heat still radiating therefrom. At a number of points, small subassemblies began to accrete as the busy tendrils brought in scattered fragments to the center of activity. Then a curved section of hull began to grow, and the tendrils, working with such frantic speed that they seemed mere blurs, hurried to transfer everything inside the space thus enclosed. Before Retief's eyes the familiar lines of the elderly craft took form, while all but a few of the tendrils worked on, inside. Those on the outside busied themselves burnishing the tarnished brightwork, at Retief's request omitting the restoration of the old pattern of scars, while removing the dents and space-dust scratches.

"Let's change the name to *Phoenix*," Retief suggested as the restorers were groping at the prow, preparing to renew the fragments of the former name. Retief wrote the new name in the dust for Pushy to scan, after which it was deftly painted on in bold script.

After an hour, Pushy withdrew the array of tendrils and reported the task completed. Retief investigated, found the interior spanking new, smelling of fresh paint, new insulation, and oiled tump leather, with which the command chair had been reupholstered.

"Fine job," he told the organism. "Remember now, don't eat the crew when the first delivery arrives. And thanks for everything."

"Farewell, Motile One," Pushy replied. "It seems a pity you could not have arrived here a few million years earlier, thus obviating a great deal of lost effort."

"I was busy evolving," Retief explained. "But no regrets: you've done a nice job of evolving yourselves into a life-form every power in the Galaxy will be eager to befriend."

"Retief," Pushy's thought came hesitantly.

"Will you come back someday? We've found your visit most stimulating."

"I shall," Retief assured the curious being. "Now stand back; this is an old-fashioned ion drive, and it could singe even you."

Chapter Four

The reconstituted *Phoenix* functioned as sweetly as she looked, lifting on command and taking up course for the tenth planet of the Barter System, Goldblatt's World, where His Ree Excellency Slive had installed his field HQ and where the time for Retief's appointment was now only hours away.

It was an uneventful transit, even the swarming Ree gunboats keeping well clear, until a hail came from a Ree dreadnaught which hove majestically into view and took up station at fifty miles on a parallel course.

"Imperial Ree flagship, Admiral Glun commanding, calling side-boat *Phoenix*," the communicater announced abruptly. "We have the honor to escort the Terran diplomatic Mission to port."

Retief acknowledged, and instructed the autopilot to lock to the Ree vessel and comply with its landing instructions.

An hour later, normal protocols thrust aside brusquely by the imperious Admiral, Retief was docked at a convenient slip adjacent to the Port Authority HQ. He descended under the watchful optical organs of a squad of Ree Rangers, conferred briefly with the maintenance personnel who reported to him, and accepted a lift in a plushed-up line cart to the office of the Port Commander.

2

The imposing building into which Retief was ushered by a punctiliously correct Ree captain and a squad of soldiers in battle dress was, it seemed, almost solid, with long, tunnel-like, mother-of-pearl-lined corridors lined with tiny cubicles, with businesslike armed sentries posted between doors. He was curtly directed into one of these.

The escorting captain saluted, a maneuver involving a curious rippling of his upper tentacular fringe, and said in barely understandable Terran:

"This is the VIP no-waiting area. The big chief don't like waiting around, Terry; he's right in there." The guide pointed to a plain door. "So you go right in and get down to business plenty chop-chop."

With that, he marched his detail off down the cramped passage. Retief entered the office of Intimidator Slive. It was a small room, its nacreous walls ornately decorated with inlays, and with a bull's eye window overlooking close-packed rooftops. Among the gold curlicues and inlays bright against the dark walls and floor, the Intimidator, standing beside his VIP ashcan, was inconspicuous, in spite of his scarlet harness and imposing height.

This upper-echelon Ree was all of six-foot-six, Retief estimated, and of commensurate girth. Like the lower-caste Ree Retief had previously encountered, his physique was a thick column of solid muscle, but on a larger scale. He inclined his garishly decorated sense-organ plate toward Retief and said in a harsh voice:

"You may enter, rash Terry, to receive your instructions."

"I already entered, and I already have my instructions, Intimidator," Retief returned firmly.

Slive recoiled a fraction of an inch and resumed:

"Since I have not yet notified you of the terms of surrender, it is obscure to me how you could have anticipated my commands relevant thereto."

"Who's surrendering?" Retief asked in mock innocence. "If you want to give up, you'd better begin by getting your advance units out of Tip space."

"You, Terry, are insolent!" Slive boomed, coming out from behind his massive desk.

"Well, I try," Retief pointed out.

"It was you, through my Groaci colleague Snith, who desired this audience," Slive pointed out. "I can conceive of no possible reason therefore other than to sign Articles of Unconditional Surrender."

"I fear Your Excellency has gotten a false impression," Retief answered. "We haven't even fought a battle yet, only a few experimental skirmishes to determine whether it will be necessary to unlock the Doom Fleet, which we naturally hold in reserve for serious occasions."

"You don't consider a confrontation with Ree might be a serious occasion?" Slive demanded in an ominous tone.

"We've been letting our military students run exercises," Retief explained. "Your fleet units make amusing targets."

He went past Slive and glanced over the U-shaped desk the Ree war-chief had vacated. The desk console, he saw, was actually a fully equipped command center. "Nice toy," he commented. "But the game's over, Slive. We've decided it's time for you to pick up what's left of your play-pretties and go home. For the present, we won't follow you and set your primitive culture back to the Stone Age."

"This," Slive stated in a voice like the first rumble of a minor earthquake, "is preposterous! You seem completely to have misconstrued the significance of our self-restrained activities!"

"That's unimportant," Retief dismissed the protest. "What's important—to your continued existence—is that you clear out of the Arm and report that the grab didn't work. This Arm is taken."

"Are you mad, Terran upstart?" Slive grated. "Consider the matter rationally, if you are indeed capable of logic: we Ree find ourselves running short of available breeding surfaces in the Western Arm; we require new worlds—and here they are, ready to pseudopod, in the adjacent Arm! And you suggest that we should forego the convenience of expanding into what is manifestly our destined sphere, merely because of the trifling circumstance that various lesser beings happen to be squatting there? It is unreasonable, Terry, can you not grasp that single fact?"

"As you state the matter, Intimidator," Retief replied thoughtfully, "it seems clear enough. But perhaps you haven't given sufficient consideration to the viewpoint of the squatters."

"What, you expect me to take into account the whims of those spoilsports? Whatever for? I fail to see how that would redound to the profit of Great Ree."

"It might help prevent a full-scale war," Retief pointed out. "So far, there've been only a few skirmishes between outlying units, doubtless exceeding orders."

"What do I care for avoiding salutary conflict?" Slive demanded. "It is clear that you Terries, no less than the perfidious Groaci, are unprepared to resist the unleashed might of Ree!"

"My point," Retief persisted, "is that if you continue to infiltrate the Arm, you'll eventually become impossible to ignore."

"We are both, presumably, beings of the world," Slive said reasonably. "Let me restate the Ree position once more, and invite your agreement that it is indeed the very soul of sweet reasonableness. Then you will of course cease your irritating interference with the orderly unfolding of Ree destiny:

"You have something we want, and we naturally intend to take it. In your possession, the worlds of the Eastern Arm serve no purpose useful to Ree; therefore, we will put them to good use. What could be more transparently equitable than that?"

"You're still overlooking the Terry position," Retief told the excited Intimidator. "Consider the case of Fred L. Underslung for example: for nearly a decade, he's been Chargé at Dobe, hanging on by his teeth and sweating out promotion at Longone. But if you fellows take over Longone, naturally we'll have broken off diplomatic relations due to the *de facto* state of war, so there'll be no ambassadorial slot there for Underslug to be appointed to. Ergo, he's against your invasion.''

"Hmmm, perhaps there's something in what you say, Terry," Slive conceded thoughtfully. "Almost, I begin to grasp the basis for your intransigence. It's an utterly novel concept, of course, to imagine that an alien might have some reason on *his* side, but this does, I confess, come close to having a certain distorted logic. However," he continued, "I foresee that if we were to yield to such yivshish, in the end it might interfere with our securing possession of your property."

"Speaking of property," Retief put in, "what about all the development the pioneers have accomplished on these outlying worlds? Mines on Hardtack and McGillicudy's World, roads and towns on Drygulch and a dozen others, farms and bridges and lumber mills, chemical plants, port facilities, golf courses and resorts, billboards, and all the rest."

"No need to fret; I assure you, that we Ree, no wastrels, will put all such amenities to good use," Slive reassured Retief. "Indeed, their existence makes the planets in question considerably more desirable than would be raw, undeveloped real estate. You see, you naively undermine your own position. But enough of these trivialities. You, Terry, will at once sign the

Articles, or suffer the consequences! I assume your simple species enjoys at least a vestigial instinct for personal preservation."

With that, the seventy-eight-inch-tall, two-foot-in-diameter cylinder of muscle advanced truculently to confront Retief.

"I've got a better idea," Retief said as the oversized Ree crowded him as if to nudge him toward the waiting window.

Retief slid aside from the thrust and, locking the massive alien's lower body with his knee, palmed the columnar being backward, toppling him to the floor, where he coiled reflexively into a stubby U-shape, and became quiescent.

Retief paused to remove the two-inch-wide blue tump-leather belt that was part of his CDT dress, service, undeveloped worlds, for use on, and strapped it around Slive's featureless torso six inches above his foot.

A full minute passed before Slive revived, struggled for purchase with his frilly 'foot,' and re-erected himself.

"Pay no attention, Terry," Slive commanded, taking no notice of the belt. "I but slipped on the floor, overzealously waxed by a menial, no doubt. But you were about to offer further concessions."

"Not quite," Retief corrected. "My idea is that if you'll pull back into your own territory, you'll save yourselves a lot of unnecessary bother."

"I don't mind a spot of bother," Slive pointed out. "Life here at Field HQ is a trifle dull, you know."

"It's livelier at the front," Retief said. "You could save a few zillion troops if you back off now."

"Whatever for? We have a gracious plenty of them. In fact, they're really why I'm here, in a way. You see," Slive went on, sounding gossipy now, "we Ree are mostly neuter. Only one egg in a thousand hatches a female and they start right in laying a million eggs a day, but there's only one male Ree. He's a horny old devil we call the Ultimate. About seven hundred years ago, standard, we had a virus epidemic that altered male genes, hormone-wise. A lot of the male population died in the epidemic. The rest were sterile—except for one male, the Ultimate. Apparently, instead of cancelling out his hormones, the virus threw all his genes into a perpetual-replacement mode. He can't die—he just goes from one longevity cycle to the next.

"So he's become the lone progenitor, and he's been busy ever since, trying to get around to *all* of those poor, lonely females, longing for the joys of motherhood.

"Once fertilized, they go on laying a million eggs a day, only now the eggs are fertile. We used to ship infertile eggs out into the Eastern Arm, under the trade name glimp eggs; seems there's a ready market for 'em, and we needed a little hard currency for paying spies and all. But we couldn't hardly ship out infant Ree the same way, the Ultimate decided. After all, they're all his own kids."

Slive paused to dab at his moist ocular patches. So," he went on, "you can see it didn't take long to fill up all our available spawning surfaces. That's why we need this Arm. These new-hatched Ree are little more than throwbacks to an early stage of Ree evolution, good for nothing but cannon-fodder. An occasional exceptional individual, such as myself, better endowed intellectually, is made an officer, to keep them headed in the right direction, with rank in accordance with IQ. We've been forced to make do with some certifiable morons. I daresay without my own dynamic leadership, the invasion would never have been launched. Most of our officer corps is wholly dependent on my direction."

"I met one of your certifiable officers," Retief said. "The idea didn't work out, it seems."

"Nope, too dumb. But we still got the spawning problem to contend with."

"Has anyone suggested to the Ultimate that he might slow down?" Retief asked.

"Are you kidding?" Slive demanded rhetorically. "It's the only fun he has and it's the basis for his exalted position besides. He'd be crazy to stop."

"Still," Retief pointed out, "there are limits to everything. The end had to come sometime, and the time is here. Just go home and report that you tried but failed."

"I don't see," Slive countered, "in what way I would explain away failure to annex available territory."

"Maybe that depends on your definition of 'available,'" Retief suggested.

"Whatever is *this* for?" Slive inquired, suddenly noticing the strap Retief had put around his lower quarters.

"I assume you want to do this thing right," Retief said. "Solemn accords should never be entered into without use of the ceremonial belt, symbolizing the binding nature of the agreement."

"Great Ree is, of course, a civilized power,"

Slive stated, deploying his neck-tentacles to adjust the belt more comfortably.

"To make it doubly binding," Retief added, "another strand around the upper quarters is considered chic. How about the drape cords?"

Eager to clinch the surrender, Slive jerked free the thick length of plush-covered rope, and deftly tied it around himself as Retief indicated, just below his tentacles.

"That's nice—and *so* flattering," Retief commented at the same moment that he stepped in close and slammed a pile-driver right hand to the Ree's pinkish nerve plexus, at which Slive instantly doubled over hard in irresistible reflex response.

Retief deftly caught the trailing end of the pull-cord and tied it firmly to the sabre-loop on the belt, cinching it up tight, forcing Slive into a tightly folded position.

The Ree Generalissimo humped on the floor, impotent, his neck-tentacles plucking ineffectively at the hard knot, Retief ignored the impotent Intimidator's bellows of rage and circled the desk to the impressive command console. At a glance he identified it as a standard Bogan export model of a type with which he was familiar from a number of previous encounters with ambitious Groaci.

While Slive yelled, Retief punched in orders to all Ree front-line units to disarm, and to disable all weaponry. The computer quickly confirmed unquestioning obedience by all units with one exception: Captain Bliff's Ree command reported, "Negative: Goblins of Goblinrock on offensive—"

Retief cut him off curtly. "This command is

direct from the HQ of Intimidator Slive," he pointed out in flawless Ree, knowing that the automatic security circuitry would instantly confirm the authenticity of the order.

Moments later, the computer reported hostile activities at the periphery of the controlled zone surrounding field HQ. A quick check confirmed that Bliff, in his frustration, had attempted to penetrate the Ree security perimeter without proper clearance and had been fired upon, precipitating a free-for-all, which automatically triggered a massive response from units of the Outer Line.

"The fools think HQ is under occupation by you Terries," Slive mourned as the volume of incoming Operational Catastrophic transmissions rose in volume and unintelligibility.

"Stop this outrage at once!" Slive yelled. "Or I shall order the instant defenestration of all Terry and other Eastern hostages, yourself taking pride of place!"

"*Au contraire*," Retief countered. "Actually, you're going to order the immediate release and repatriation of all your state guests. Start with the ones you turned over to the Groaci Consul, Snith. I'll give you access to your gameboard here long enough for that. Any argument or delay, and I'll have to see just how sensitive that yatz-patch of yours is: say a good hard kick to start with, with a furb-ache thrown in for good measure."

"The highly-evolved Ree organism cannot servive mistreatment of the nexus," Slive stated coldly. "The barbarity you threaten would leave you incarcerated here with a corpse, and no way out. I suggest, out of sheer great-heartedness, that you reconsider. You got in, Terry, thanks to my punctilious observation of protocol, but how will you return to your own?"

Without a word, Retief went to the single round window, released the latch, and swung the hinged frame open. Even at this height, the wind gust bore a faint aroma of rotting refuse.

"I take it this is the window you planned to throw me out of," he commented, "since it's the only one I've seen in your hive, and it seems to have been installed very recently." He touched the still-damp mortar securing the porthole-like window.

"Correct," Slive conceded. "We Ree evolved from a handsome molluscoid form, you know; for ages we secreted our own personal chambers, which lacked windows. Ergo, we now feel no need overly to be reminded of vast chasms of open space yawning below us."

"Nice view," Retief commented. He leaned out and surveyed the sheer drop to a paved courtyard a thousand feet below. Slive shuddered. Retief examined the expanse of coarsely stuccoed wall looming above another fifty feet to an overhanging cornice, then turned back to Slive, whose hide had faded to a sickly greenish color.

"You don't like windows much, do you, Slive?" Retief inquired rhetorically. "Suppose I just push you out this one?"

The Intimidator spasmed convulsively. "Not that, Terry! Such a fate is beyond contemplation! Perhaps some accommodation could be worked out!"

"Too late," Retief said sadly. "I'm mad now."

He put one leg out, groped, and found a foot-hold on the rough surface.

"So long, ex-Intimidator," he called cheerfully to the immobilized war-lord. "Maybe within a few weeks one of your well-briefed underlings will get up his nerve to come in and see why you've been so quiet, and then you'll have the fun of explaining what happened. You can tell them I went out the window on schedule, which should help to establish your reputation all over again from scratch; but that shouldn't bother you much; I hear it only took you thirty years the first time."

Retief paused and scanned the sky, where ragged formations of Ree warcraft were converging from all directions at bombing altitude. Even as he watched, the first stick of chemical warheads fell away from the lead craft, followed almost at once by the deep-toned *crum-mp-p*! of detonation, which sent up a cloud of dense brown smoke from the outskirts of town to shred in the wind as more bombs fell, and more, their points of impact advancing steadily across the city.

"That's assuming there's anybody left alive to release you," he added to his gloomy prediction.

Slive humped on the floor, yelling curses.

"Your staff will assume you're giving the impudent Terry a good going-over," Retief suggested. "Of course, you *could* forget about losing face and yell for help."

"You, too, shall die in the holocaust, mischievous Terry!" Slive warned. "For Mug's sake, Retief, call 'em off! Let me at that console for ten seconds and prevent tragedy: I've got a locked channel that can cut through ten layers of jam-

ming and override any priority up to Imperial
Whim! Only just lay off that window!"

Slive strained in vain against his bonds, tentacles slack now, his hoarse voice fading to a
whimper.

At that moment a near-miss threw a hail of
shrapnel against the wall close enough for a
sliver to draw blood from Retief's exposed ankle.
He climbed back inside, went to the fallen big
shot, took a grip on the leather belt, which was
biting deep into the CIIU's muscular torso, and
dragged him behind the console.

"First, order the hostages freed," he instructed.
"Then you can call off the attack."

Slive flipped keys with his tentacles, shouting
against the incomprehensible bellow from the
tight-security, top-priority channels, the bedlam
now amplified by the impact of bombs near at
hand. The building shuddered.

"—at me!" Slive was yelling. "Abort mission!
You have been duped by the enemy! Break off
attack immediately and return to station! Clear
classified channels for incoming Operational Ultimate orders! I repeat: break off attack at once!"

As his voice faded, cracked and became a mere
croak, the volume of incoming calls slowly faded,
only an occasional word or phrase coming
through:

"Foul-up! But I've got my orders . . ."

"—old Slive says hit HQ, he don't mean head
for the boondocks!"

"—emergency plan twelve-point-oh-nine. Clear
enough. But—"

"Knock it off, I said!" Slive yelled raggedly,
flipping keys frantically.

The attack formations were dispersing reluctantly, Retief saw through the shrapnel-shattered glass. Slive whimpered, his tentacles slack.

"Now the hostages," Retief reminded his host. He came over to stand beside the trussed-up Ree chieftain, who attempted to writhe out of reach of a kick to the yatz-patch. Retief jerked him back into optimum position, prodded the pink area with his toe.

"All right, all right," Slive croaked. "I got to give the old laryngeal plates a little rest first," he whispered, breaking off to cough rackingly.

"Now!" Retief said and drew back his foot. Slive began operating a different row of keys, marked in obscure Ree glyphs.

"All stations," he grated, "the signing of a new Ree-Terra accord renders status of hostages equivocal."

He paused. "I can make this a kill order just as easy, Terry," he told Retief. "You've got to ante up again. Now, what I've got in mind: I turn this bunch of nobodies loose, and you Terries deliver a new set, only VIP's this time. Better make up your mind, Terry." Slive turned back to his command console.

"Hold it," Retief said quickly. "No kill order. I'm not empowered to offer you any substitutes, except one. Me. Free the hostages, and one month from today, after I've personally confirmed that the hostages are home safe, I'll come back and report to you."

"Done!" Slive cried. "A capital notion, Terry! What fun I shall have with you ere I cast your broken remains out that selfsame window!" With renewed vigor, the CIIU resumed his tight-beam transmission to all Reedom:

"Contingency plan 321," he cited. "Release hostages intact, and deliver them to the nearest Terry enclave! I want them turned over in good shape, so nobody can claim that Great Ree don't know how to treat its property! Do it!"

"Get Snith on the hotline," Retief ordered. "Tell him to put Hardtack's Governor Anderson on." A moment later, he heard the elderly hostage's cracked voice.

". . . tell this five-eyed little plucked rooster what—"

"Never mind, Governor," Retief said soothingly. "Keep cool and you'll be on your way to Hardtack within the hour. Spread the word: It's a genuine repatriation; we've worked out a deal."

"Wouldn't trust none of them consarned worms as far as they can jump," Anderson complained, until Retief signed off.

"Now what, bold Terry?" Slive demanded. "What, pray, is to prevent me from ordering my troops in to defenestrate you as originally planned?"

"Don't waste their time," Retief suggested, going to the window. "We Terries evolved from an aboreal type, you know. We love a brisk climb before dinner."

He swung himself out and was pleased to find convenient new hand-and-footholds where patches of stucco had been knocked away by the same blast which had broken the glass.

He leaned back in to wave to Slive, and started the upward climb. A soldier on an adjacent rooftop noticed and fired an offhand shot which knocked a chunk from the cornice in a convenient place to assist the lone Terran in gaining the roof.

Once there, Retief quickly sought out the stairhead, opened the heavy hatch-cover, and descended into the now familiar fishy odor. Down the dim, nacreous stairwell, he could hear faint sounds of alarms and excursions below. A glow from one side indicated the mouth of a cross-passage, which he entered and followed to the wider and relatively well-lit main corridor. Here he waited for a squad of uniformed Ree soldiery to pass, escorting a gaunt and ragged Terran, who shuffled along the corridor, shoulders hunched, muttering.

"—mess up a fellow's nap," he was uttering to himself aggrievedly. "Coulda waited a while. . . ."

Retief went along to the lift by which the group had arrived, rode it down to ground level, where he was challenged at once by a guard with the broad belly-stripes of a sergeant, who made an abortive move toward his holstered hand-gun, then waved him on.

"I've seen this one before; Admiral, said VIP treatment all the way," he explained to a pair of lesser sentries who had hurried forward, eager to exercise petty authority.

Without further incident, Retief reached the street, commandeered the passenger compartment of the same vehicle in which he had arrived, which was still parked in the GENERAL OFFICERS slot, and ordered the somnolent driver to take him to the port.

"Figgered yer worship to be in there longer," the chauffuer carped, laying aside his comic book. "Figgered I was good for the afternoon." Retief handed him a ten-Guck note to assuage his sorrow, and was rewarded with a fast trip to the CREW gate. Here he permitted the helpful driver to use his special key on the heavy padlock, and proceeded to the READY zone, where he briskly selected a line-cart and drove it across the cracked ramp to the berth assigned to *Phoenix*. As he opened the entry port, a cop-cart arrived and squealed to a halt.

"Oh, for a minute I thought you was one of them Terries," the officer-braided policeman explained. "But that don't add up because nobody leaves those fellows running loose. I heard His Ex is planning to do some kinda swap deal. This here is a Terry boat, though, so you must be from the Eastern Arm, right? So I guess you must be one o' them Groacs or whatever. Never could understand why you fellows sold out your own Arm, no offense."

"To abstain from feckless speculation, Chief Inspector," Retief replied in flawless Groaci. "To extend my compliments to the Chief of Operations, and inform him I shall lift at once and require close escort to the vicinity of Goblinrock."

"Oh, sure, chief, I mean yer highness or whatever the appropriate style is fer foreign big shots."

As soon as *Phoenix* was clear of the ground-clutter, a tight formation of Ree gunships formed up to englobe completely the departing vessel, intercepting and warning off the patrol boats which swarmed to investigate the unscheduled liftoff.

Retief monitored the exchange of conversation on the open band, and after keying in his course, ate a light meal of *boeuf bourgignon* and a delicate Chablis, then went aft for a nap. As he dozed off he heard a commanding Ree voice cut through the background chatter:

"Now hear our sublime Intimidator Slive!" it announced impressively; then the voice of Slive himself: "From the depths of our inscrutable wisdom, we have determined that it is expedient that the recently dismissed Envoy of Terra, one Retief, be detained for further interrogation."

Slive's voice increased its decibels. "All units! Seize the Terran ship *Phoenix*. Don't destroy! Deliver the unspeakable Retief in prime condition for most intense interrogation!"

The open radio band seemed to vibrate with harsh echoes.

Noting that Goblinrock now lay a fractional AU dead ahead, Retief reached out tentatively with the insubstantial voice he had fallen so easily into using with the native organism on that body:

"Pushy—I'm estimating planet-fall in plus nine-oh-three-one, mark. Your next big meal is following me in."

"Greeting, Retief," Pushy's reply came promptly. "Welcome back! And we appreciate your thoughtfulness in bringing lunch. We do hope it's still alive, thus to furnish us the fun of preparing our meal personally."

Retief reassured the alien that the Ree would arrive alive and full of determination to retain that status.

"Superb!" Pushy came back. "Good sport, as well as good eats! Capital. Do hurry!"

Retief landed his refurbished ship on the opposite side of the small world from his first contact, but found Pushy, now resembling a heap of violet soccer balls, awaiting him.

Before he had finished telling Pushy what had been happening to him, a Ree cruiser flashed overhead, followed a moment later by three squadrons of atmospheric craft, a detachment of which peeled off to settle in in a mile-wide circle around *Phoenix* and Pushy.

"Oh goody," Pushy interrupted, "lunchtime!"

At once he collapsed into a heap of unconnected spheres, each of which rolled off on its own, forming a thin, purple circle, expanding like a ring on water to contact and overwhelm each Ree fighter craft as it fruitlessly fired anti-personnel charges at the advancing balls.

Retief tuned to the Ree battle-command frequency and overheard the confused babble:

"—new trick! What—hold it! Belay that! Secure all hatches with manual safe-bars!"

"—already told you slobs, deploy anti-explosive barriers and firewalls! Don't let—"

"—pigtail three to pigtail one, over! Pigtail three—"

"—have your orders," an overriding transmission cut through the gobble. "I shall dock and establish my field HQ at locus 13 degrees north, zero latitude. Stand by for further instructions."

"—tried everything! This stuff is everywhere, like sticky fish-nets, and it keeps coming! Ouch, it—"

"Silence!" the commanding voice boomed out. "We are now in position and can observe a curious phenomenon. G-5, did you report violet cobwebs? You blundered: these cobwebs are of a distinct green tint! We are now declaring a Condition Scarlet alert! Stand by!"

As the last Ree transmission cut off abruptly, Retief noticed that the purple spheres had reassembled and were even now taking the form of a lone, snow-white column, reaching far up into Goblinrock's dark sky.

"Capital!" Pushy exclaimed suddenly. "Retief, this has been an occasion of great joy. I didn't waste any H_2O on these fellows, just bathed them in HCl; they dissolved readily. How soon can we hope for another shipment?"

"Not before your appetite recovers, I trust," Retief suggested. "I'd like to stay and visit, but I have to be on my way, before someone back at Sector gives away the Eastern Arm. Ta."

Chapter Five

Back in Space, Retief found that all Ree military craft had withdrawn to extreme radio range, their traffic, coming through faintly amid a background of star static, being concerned with such topics as 'orderly withdrawal,' 'tight quarantine,' and 'Terry secret weapons.'

He bypassed Prute and the other outlying Fringe worlds, and headed in-Arm at flank speed. M'hu hu's refurbished tramp had the high-speed capability to be expected of a former attack destroyer. He was passed inward without comment by the TSA pickets, and at a fractional AU from Aldo, he made contact via tight beam with Sector HQ in the person of Undersecretary Clayfoot, the Staff Duty Officer, and transmitted a concise report on his mission to Slive.

"I had to twist the Intimidator's furb," Retief concluded, "but he agreed to exchange all the Terran hostages for one VIP from the *Corps Diplomatique*, namely me. I'm to return in one standard month, after I've made sure the hostages are safe."

"You say your name is Retief?" Clayfoot cut in peremptorily.

"Can't be," another voice in the background commented. "That's that fellow—the trouble-maker; Crodfoller sent him off on a suicide mission. Must be a hoax."

"Never mind, George," Clayfoot's glutinous voice responded, off-mike. "I'll just pump the hoaxer a bit, and find out something useful. Now, let's just scan this so-called report. Hmmm, proposes to exchange diplomats for dirt farmers; pedants for peasants, unlikely on the face of it. Here, fellow: how many senior CDT officials did you say they're demanding in return for, let me see, one hundred twenty distressed colonists?"

"Just one, Mr. Secretary, me," Retief replied patiently.

"That's absurd!" Clayfoot snapped. "Even if we considered one bureaucrat for ten bucolics a fair rate of exchange, that would be an even dozen. And you say they're only asking for a mere Second Secretary of Embassy and Consul; preposterous! You betray your lack of knowl-edge of great affairs, fellow! Now, give up this imposture and clear the channel for important matters!"

"I was pressed for time," Retief informed his superior. "I didn't wait around to negotiate a less favorable exchange ratio."

"Indeed! Now, Mr. Retief or whatever your actual identity may be, I shall now test your *bona fides* by a few questions regarding matters known only to a select few inner-circle officers here at Sector: What's on the menu for next Tuesday at the Officer's Open Mess?"

"Gerbil-culture burgers, Ka-swe, cultured hundred-year cug, peanut-butter and olive salad, and authentic Chicago smörgåsar," Retief replied promptly, suppressing an impulse to gag.

"I can see the rot runs deep," Clayfoot said to his unseen companion, "the rascal knows his eats."

"Probably bribed Jerry, the bartender at the VIP lounge," the background voice suggested.

"By no means," Retief corrected. "The menus for March were on page two of the *Daily Corps* last week."

"By Jove, perhaps this Retief really *did* make the *gaffe* of returning from a one-way assignment," Clayfoot muttered. "Damned inconvenient. I've already assigned a new man to complete the iceberg count out on Icebox Nine. Now, see here, Retief," he went on, addressing the microphone directly:

"You're to keep this strictly confidential; not a word to anyone until I've debriefed you! Is that understood?"

"It's jake at this end, Mr. Secretary," Retief reassured the great man. "I'm estimating Aldo in plus twelve-ten-two. I could use a meal and a bed before debriefing, if the tactical situation allows."

"Good notion, Retief! I follow your thinking: if you were rushed direct to the Staff Duty Office, rumors might spread that you had Hot Dope— and we wouldn't want that, eh?"

2

Phoenix docked precisely on schedule, and Retief emerged to be met by an Embassy driver, who whisked him to HQ at a speed well in excess of the limit established by Regulations.

He was at once assigned a spartan chamber in the Diplomatic Officers Quarters and had removed his shoes and stretched out when a cautious tapping sounded at the door. He opened it and Ben Magnan scurried in.

"Gracious," Magnan whispered. "I mustn't be seen here, Retief! It's top hush-hush, but when I heard that you'd actually come alive through a meeting with CIIU Slive, naturally I had to see you at once. Candidly, I feared for you—for, in spite of all, I have a feeling that without your peculiar style of diplomacy, the CDT would be the poorer. Welcome back!"

Retief accepted the excited Econ man's handshake and reassured him that Intimidator Slive had turned out to be a reasonable chap after all.

"Rumors are flying, Retief," Magnan reported breathlessly. "Somehow Jerry—the barman, you know—got wind of some immense plum of an assignment that's become available to a few select headquarters types, a result of your own dealings with the Chief Intimidator, the story has it. Perhaps I myself might aspire to be one of these Special Delegates, Jerry says. If you could give me the inside dope, Retief, that might just swing the balance in my favor. Surely, as an old associate, you'll give that edge, eh?"

"I suggest, Mr. Magnan," Retief replied "that you let this particular plum go to some older, more deserving fellows. It's likely to be a once-in-a-lifetime experience. I don't think you're ready for it."

3

When the majestic bulk of the august personage known to his underlings as Deputy Undersecretary Shortfall, and to his superiors as Tubby,
had seated himself with a ponderous gravity
reminiscent of the settling of the foundations of
Boulder Dam, and had cleared his throat like
the premonitory rumbling of a Richter 9 earthquake, the great man spoke:

"Well, fellows, I suppose you've all heard the
rumors of fantastically desirable assignments
coming up for a few lucky chaps upon whom
Fate and the Corps smile. The rumors, gentlemen are, in a word, true. And this morning it is
my grave and solemn responsibility to desig-
nate those to whom this plum will fall. Proudfoot . . ." Shortfall paused to turn a benign and
slightly bleary eye on the assistant Political
Officer, who looked bright-eyed and sat erect,
"you, of course, are far too junior to fall within
the zone of consideration."

His gaze drifted to Career Ambassador Sidesaddle: "Now, Mr. Ambassador, you, on the other
hand, with your vast field experience, merited
serious consideration. Too bad most of your missions rated a big X in the 'Dismal Failure' column on your annual rating sheet. So let us pass
on to . . . hmmm, where is the fellow? Ah, there
you are, Hencrate. Not trying to hide behind
Marvin, are you?"

"I'm skinny, sir," Hencrate said unhappily. "I
was just trying not to look obtrusive."

"I shall overlook your excessive modesty this
time, Hank," the great man said in a tone of Heavy
Indulgence (231-w). "I can tell you now that you
are First Alternate on the Delegation of Honor."

He paused for the spontaneous applause and congratulatory cries to subside.

"Now, on to matters of more moment. Hencrate, Lackluster, Underthrust, Tumblehome, Ajax—you gentlemen are our first-line selections. Your team leader will be Career Minister Homer Sitzfleisch, a Galaxy-class diplomat whom I know you all revere." Again, faint cries and a spattering of handclaps sounded.

"Now, you chaps selected as Special Aides and Attachés—let me see . . ." Short-fall muttered as he peered along the table over the tops of the Ben Franklin spectacles he affected, "—ah, yes, all present, I see, as well as a number of excessively optimistic fellows. The following will kindly leave the room—"

He tolled off the names of those eliminated, who dutifully and in silence filed from the chamber of the elect. The chosen few, relaxing a bit now that they knew they were *in*, listened almost casually as the rest of the names of the designated were called out.

"Now, gentlemen," the Deputy Undersecretary summed up, "to you has fallen a proud and perilous honor: yes, perilous, gentlemen; we may as well face it: perilous because on your success rests the future of Ree-Terran relations for the next few millennia, at least, and the danger of failure is real. But all of you, I am persuaded, are of a stature equal to the challenge. You've already had your GUTS priority pre-orientation, and I now hand you your Cosmic-Category final briefing kits."

He paused to unstrap an unwieldy briefcase of the type in which ambitious junior executives carry their lunch, and distributed pink-jacketed booklets.

"What's this about 'ceremonial leg-irons'?" Underthrust demanded after a glance at his pamphlet.

"A trifling formality," Shortfall explained. "A token nod to Ree custom. In the code of these primitive, ah, emergent, uh, developing . . . inferior, that is, folk, the wearing of the comfy, light-weight, handsomely damascened shackles symbolizes acceptance of Ree dominance. A sop to their egos, Underthrust.

"Now, as to the section detailing appropriate modes of address to Ree dignitaries, we must, of course, as professionals overlook the superficially demeaning implications of saying: 'This inferior tool of a decadent tyranny abjectly supplicates his Galactic honor the Intimidator,' et cetera, et cetera. Doesn't mean a thing: it's like calling someone 'Mister,' that is, 'Master,' with no actual implications of slavery.

"Oh, yes, I meant to add that a fellow named Retief will be going along as a sort of guide; over my objections, actually; still, he's been there before and may possibly prove of some use. Gentlemen, if there are no questions—" he paused to show the assembled honorees an expression which strongly suggested that there had better not be—

"The meeting is concluded. Wear your new laurels lightly, fellows. Those of you who survive the experience—all of you, I meant to say—will no doubt receive appropriate notations on your next ER."

"Lordy," a starry-eyed Budget and Fiscal man in from Krako Six murmured. "Just having the privilege of sitting at his feet is an education in sophisticated Nullspeak. Over a thousand cogent and syntactically faultless words, and he commits himself and the Department to absolutely nothing."

"He did *not*," the portly Political Officer on his left objected in a whisper. "He distinctly said there'd be promos all around when we get back!"

"Hardly, Cedric," the Undersecretary corrected quietly. "I fear high-level Nullspeak is wasted on certain individuals."

"I didn't mean," Cedric protested. "I only meant—"

"Now you're getting the idea," Shortfall encouraged his subordinate. "Never forget the stirring admonition of AE and MP Slipshod, reveeered be his remains, wherever they may be."

"Sure, but what was the stirring admonition and all?" someone wondered aloud, then went on: "Oh, I remember: that was the one about 'The implication is mightier than the affadavit.' Right, boss?"

"Pack carefully, gentlemen," Shortfall admonished his flock as he rose and moved to the door. "No need to burden yourselves with excessive reserves of denture-cleaner and rug-adhesive, since within the month you shall be either on your way home, triumphant, or entered on the roll of Those Who Gave Their All in the line of duty. Gentlemen, I salute you." With a final flip of his hand, the Deputy Undersecretary departed.

As if a conversational dam had burst, a babble of conversation broke out at once, quickly diminishing in effusiveness as the proximity of the great man, and the likelihood of being overheard diminished.

"—laying it on the line!"

"—the privilege of participating in the briefing, alone!"

"—did he mean by that last crack, 'Gave Their All,' huh?"

"—a mere figure of speech. Can't say he didn't warn us."

"What about this tourist guide wallah he mentioned?"

"—ask him a few questions."

"Now, gentlemen," Homer Sitzfleisch, as Team Leader designee, spoke up in mild reproof. "Every assignment has both its positive and its negative aspects. I suggest, indeed direct, that we concentrate our attention on the former. You noted that when Cedric mentioned that we'd all been promised promotions, the Undersecretary didn't actually *deny* it."

"He said 'hardly,' " Underthrust countered bleakly.

"You're just not used to the subtleties of Nullspeak," Sitzfleisch reproved his junior. "After all, why does the language possess such expressions as 'maybe,' 'in a sense,' 'perhaps,' 'about,' 'more than,' 'almost,' and so on? To enable us to communicate at a more delicate level, commitment-wise," he answered his own rhetorical query. "Now, chaps, let's get over to Supply and draw our special issue, as it says here in the folder."

"I still got my doubts," Underthrust muttered. "If it's such a choice trip, how come old Short-fall's not going himself?"

4

"What's all the hassle?" the chinless lad assigned as assistant to the HQ Chief Clerk, Message Center, inquired of his boss, a paunchy little man with an offensively silky manner, and mustache to match.

"Not to worry, Cricket, my boy," the chief urged his minion. "Just another tempest in a chamber pot, I'm sure. Routine personnel action, nothing more."

"OK, boss," Cricket replied. "I guess I got no call to put in for overtime to try to get this stuff off to Central Record Control ahead of the semi-annual requisitions. I already got about a car-load of them, and more still coming in."

"No item for overtime pay was included in my last budget estimate, dear boy," the chief clerk pointed out stiffly. "Thus, clearly, the proposal is out of order. Get the Requisition collated and dispatched at once. You know how fussy General Services is about timely submission. Never mind about the queries that have been coming in from Preliminary Review. It's none of our business if certain posts are calling for hand-guns instead of hand-lotion, and flame-throwers in place of flame retardants."

"Yeah, but," Cricket objected feebly. "And I was meaning to ask you: Is it OK if I let a CDTO-2 help me out? Fella was in the office looking up some stuff when the fecal matter encountered the air-distribution system, and he gave me a hand sorting out stuff like these here personnel actions, transfers and like that; routine, like you said."

"I myself cleared Mr. Retief to enter the vaults," the pot-bellied chief clerk replied grandly. "Has a right to, you know. CDTM-1-23A sub-paragraph two b, on Review of Records, covers it."

Chapter Six

After leaving the prison-like confines of the Message Center, Retief reported to the Transportation Officer, who provided him with documentation covering the requisition of the unregistered de-commissioned Class III vessel *Phoenix* for official use on a non-compensatory basis, reassignment of the vessel to Retief as Administrative Assistant assigned to Special Mission Number One, handed over a heavy volume of Intelligence data regarding Ree Field Headquarters at Barter Nine, and added his advice:

"Better keep a low profile, Retief; you're nursemaiding a load of top brass such as I've never seen since the last time the Secretary threw a birthday party, back at the Department on Terra."

"I'll try to keep them headed in the right direction, Fred," Retief assured the admin chief.

2

Arriving at the port a few hours later, Retief was met, not to say confronted, by no less a personage than Special Envoy Sitzfleisch.

"Here, you're that fellow Retief," the Team Leader charged.

"Guilty," Retief replied.

"Time to get this show on the road," Sitzfleisch stated. "Now, you're supposed to know how to find this confounded fellow Slive, His Excellency the Chief Intimidator, I mean, and by the way, no crew has yet reported for duty, I'm informed."

"That's in order, sir," Retief reassured the TL. "I'm checked out on this type. She's a Z-type, designed for operation by minimal crew. So we can load at once. I've filed the flight plan with Ops."

"The members of my Special Team are already aboard," the AE and MP replied shortly. "I was merely awaiting your own arrival to order lift-off."

"We're tight-scheduled for oh-nineteen hundred, half an hour yet," Retief pointed out. "Ops would take a dim view of anyone trying to jump the launch order, especially without the authorization of the rated deep space pilot."

"Don't let that 'pilot' stuff go to your head, Mr. Retief," Sitzfleisch rebuked his subordinate sharply. "I am Team Leader; you're merely a nondiplomatic admin chap here. *I* give the orders."

"That being the case, Mr. Ambassador," Retief replied, "CDT regs require that you qualify yourself as a rated pilot and so register with Operations."

"Nonsense, I'm no bus driver!" Sitzfleisch snapped. "You can take care of all that sort of thing, of course. Now, what's the low-down, Retief? I hear you've visited this chap Slive; what's he really like?"

"He's a cruel, ambitious thug," Retief told him, "but on the other hand, he's a liar and a swindler."

"Are you saying the fellow is a career diplomat?" the TL demanded.

"You said that," Retief pointed out. "So don't quote me."

3

An hour later, *Phoenix* was on course for Fringe Space at flank speed, and already her complement of Retief and twelve senior bureaucrats had settled into the monotonous routine of deep-space travel.

Bypassing Goblinrock, Retief conferred briefly with Pushy via the latter's unconventional direct-link technique.

"Pity," the totipotent being commented when Retief told him he wouldn't be landing this trip. "But we've learned patience over the ages, and of course we're well fed at the moment and full of new ideas. Do stop in again soon, and I'll tell you all about our new project."

"Don't start yet," Retief cautioned. "I think I can promise you a steady supply of glimp eggs, starting very soon now. Meanwhile, don't do anything to upset the *status quo*."

Pushy agreed to allow his grandiose new

schemes to lie fallow for the present, and abruptly lapsed into the comatose state which, he had explained, helped pass the eons with minimal ennui.

4

Nearing the Goober Cluster, Retief programmed a course correction to bring the speedy vessel into landing orbit at the sparsely-settled world officially designated RNGCA6321, but known to its hardy inhabitants as Hardtack.

As the converted destroyer took up its parking orbit, Retief tuned the communicator to the local traffic band, and was instantly assailed by a clamor of voices, all talking at once, and all, it seemed at the top of their lungs.

"—got the sucker in my sights—"

"—save some for Y Squadron!"

"—told you bums to stand by for orders!" a domineering voice cut through the babble. "Whattya think this is? A wild barf-beast hunt or something? Now, B Squadron, you fall in, in echelon left like the plan calls for, and the rest o' you—"

"—no exercise! Let's go get 'em!"

At the same moment, the long-range proximity detectors *ping*!ed imperatively.

"What is it?" Homer Sitzfleisch demanded, peering over Retief's shoulder at the screen which displayed an irregular array of small objects converging on Phoenix. "A meteor swarm?" The Team Leader hazarded. "Odd sort of phenomenon to find orbiting a T-class planet."

"I think it's our reception committee," Retief replied.

"Impossible!" Sitzfleisch snapped. "I notified no one of our anticipated arrival! In fact, I myself was not aware you planned to detour to this benighted frontier post. What explaiation do you offer?"

"Hardtack One, *Phoenix* calling," Retief said into the extreme range talker. "Kindly organize yourselves to escort a CDT vessel transporting a party of VIP's on an Operational Cosmic Urgent mission."

"Looks like the boys are on the ball," he added, addressing Sitzfleisch. Abruptly, the incoherent clamor of incomings cut off, and a commanding voice came through clearly:

"CDT *Phoenix*, Hardtack One here. We were notified you'd be coming, but we didn't exactly believe it. Just give me a minute here, and I'll whip this bunch of mine into shape. By the way, hold your fire if some of my eager beavers happen to let off a few ranging shots. Don't worry, they'll probably miss."

"What's that?" Sitzfleisch demanded. "We're to be fired on? By Terran colonists? Return fire, Mr. Retief, and do so at once."

"You'd better go lie down, Mr. Ambassador," Retief suggested quietly. "We've penetrated their outer perimeter, it seems, without proper clearance, so the boys are understandably excited. But our automatics can take care of any stray rounds that happen to come our way.

"Roger, Hardtack One," he said into the talker. "Request escort for immediate docking at your main port."

"Roger, CDT," Hardtack came back. "I can get you down right away; as for our main port, we only got the one. Over and out."

On the forward and lateral screens, the horde of small craft which had risen to challenge the intruder were closing in, some firing as they came.

"We'll be blasted to atoms!" Sitzfleisch yelled. "Mr. Retief, I suggest—nay, I *command* that you return fire at once!"

"Very well, Mr. Ambassador," Retief said calmly. "Could you assist by pushing the missile buttons?"

"With pleasure, Retief," Sitzfleisch said, moving to the Attack console.

"No, not those missiles. They're long-range," Retief said, directing him to a shiny metal box with rows of black buttons.

The Team Leader jabbed his finger enthusiastically at a sequence of buttons.

Retief turned back to the battle screens. The swarm of attacking ships was thinning.

There was an interruption at the rear of the Control Center. A junior political officer poked his head around the edge of the entry panel and complained, "The chiefs back here want to know what's going on. Who's monkeying with the music tapes? The sound is jumping from octave to octave—"

The junior nodded and withdrew.

Sitzfleisch had stopped jabbing the stereo buttons and was watching the screens. The last attacker veered off at contact minus a fractional second.

The babble of excited voices incoming on the local band thinned out, to be dominated at last by the emphatic commands of Hardtack One:

"Form escort of honor to convoy CDT vessel

now in transfer orbit on no-budget straight-line approach to position 1-A. Then all unit commanders will report to me in my office on the double. Second officers, stand by for further instructions."

"Well," the Team Leader commented with satisfaction, "we brought the frontier beggars to their senses."

Inquisitive members of the Select team now crowded into the Control Center. Sitzfleisch included them in his observations. "By the way, prepare yourselves for our formal reception; within the hour: class ones, medals and orders. We're descending to the surface of a body locally known as Hardtack."

"I've heard of it," a round-shouldered Admin type commented tonelessly. "Nothing good. Expect the blighters know nothing of protocol."

"Yep," a string-thin Budget and Fiscal man agreed. "Understand the place is a *de facto* penal colony, founded by two shiploads of incorrigibles from all over Tip Space."

"Shouldn't wonder," a plump Information Service Attaché contributed. "Why honor these guttersnipes with a visit?"

"Actually," the Team Leader put in, "these fellows would be the grandchildren of the guttersnipes. Seem to have worked out at least a crude sort of system of law and order. Perhaps we shan't be wasting our time completely."

Retief advised the excited diplomats to strap in securely, and returned his attention to the monitor screens. The local craft, all converted civilian vessels, ranging in size from heavy cargo transports to private pleasure craft, had again englobed the visitor and formed up in the traditional "fountain" formation, with a steady flow of units changing position in the convoy from advance section to rearguard, a technique designed for maximum survival potential in the event of surprise attack.

"Seems they don't trust us," commented the lieutenant general who was the sole military representative on the Special Team. "That fountain formation is ordinarily used for escort of a captive capital ship by an inferior force. Can't say I blame 'em; this tub could blow 'em out of space with one volley, if we weren't friendly."

"Good idea, Bob," Team Leader Sitzfleisch said briskly. "Mr. Retief, I've changed my mind. I hereby order you to open fire and clear these rabble out of here."

"That might be hard for Your Excellency to explain as an amiable gesture to the ground batteries that are no doubt zeroed in on us by now, Mr. Ambassador," Retief demurred. "And when they listen to the tapes back at the Department, it's possible that someone might even utter the dread word 'isolationist,' not to say 'warmonger.'"

"Perish the thought, my boy," Sitzfleisch purred. "Suppose something went wrong with the recorders, here in the command compartment: I don't suppose you could fix it in time to catch my joking remarks about opening fire, just now."

"The retrogressive capabilities of the equipment are minimal," Retief reassured the flustered TL. "Suppose we proceed with our preparations for the reception, as Your Excellency so perceptively suggested."

"Capital notion," Sitzfleisch breathed, mopping at his forehead with a large floral-patterned tissue.

5

When the *ping*!ing of gradually cooling, entry-seared hot metal had ceased, a lantern-jawed man casually uniformed in blue-dyed homespun ornamented with an amount of buttons and braid suggestive of Field Marshal rank advanced to the *Phoenix*'s landing party in a studied saunter.

"All right, fellows, I'm Sergeant-Major Grundy," he announced in a brassy voice. "Which one of you boys is in charge here?"

"May I present Ambassador Sitzfleisch," Retief spoke up as the latter bustled forward to confront his host.

"Only a sergeant?" Sitzfleisch muttered as he started to offer a handshake, then patted his paunch instead. "A mere non-com to meet me and my little party of heroes—none of whom is less than a CDTO-10, except for my driver Retief, of course."

"Happens Sergeant-Major's the top dog in our organization," Grundy snapped. "Now, what's the idea getting our fellows all stirred up? Figgered it was another Ree invasion."

"It so happens, Sergeant," the Team Leader replied coldly, "that I am on a mission of the utmost gravity, and it was only with reluctance that I decided to honor your small planet with an actual State Visit."

"Gosh," Grundy said expressionlessly.

"According to the CDT List," Underthrust put in, "there's a Consulate here. Where's the Consul?"

"I was about to inquire as to that," Team Leader Ambassador Sitzfleisch said quickly. "Damned odd the fellow's not here, eh?"

"Nope," Grundy said. "Be pretty strange if he *was* here, seein's he took off right after the Rees hit the Plantation and grabbed the governor and all."

"Impossible!" Sitzfleisch thundered. "A diplomat deserting his post in the face of the, ah, alleged enemy."

"Maybe he heard *you* was coming, Cap'n," Grundy suggested expressionlessly. "And there ain't nothing 'alleged' about the enemy. Them suckers burned our *en*tire zitz-weed crop, and our snick berries didn't come out too good, neither, seein's they parked their go-boats right in the midst of our prime acreage. You watch: snick berries are going skyhigh. That's a market tip, fellows. Well, are we going to stand here and jaw the whole day, or are we going up to town and have some eats? We got a kind of lash-up banquet laid on, soon's we heard we bagged us a boatload of big shots from Aldo."

"A modest meal would not be amiss," Sitzfleisch conceded, amidst the enthusiastic cries of his subordinates:

"—some real chow at last!"

"—one's palate is probably atrophied!"

"—shipboard rations! Never—"

"Ah, just what are you serving, Sergeant Major?" the Team Leader inquired.

"Got a big rock ranger, that's a local sheep," Grundy replied. "Kinda gamey if you ain't used to it. Descended from goats and sheep the early explorers turned loose here. Smells pretty bad. Tough, too, a big old male like this is. But like the little fellow said, it's better'n x-rations. Got some fine gravy with it, too. We pour that over the mashed bile-tarnips. Hope you like bichy-bichy, about a hundred-ninety proof, got plenty of that, made outa local lichen you know, little green, but plenty of vitamins. For dessert, well, I guess there won't be no dessert, cause the batch the Eady boys was bringing done blowed up on 'em. Too much yeast, I guess, and a mutated strain at that. Let's go."

As Grundy completed his description of the viands in store, a knock-kneed flatbed pulled up alongside the little group in a cloud of powdered guano, and the Sergeant Major waved his guests aboard, but caught Retief's eye.

"Seein's you're the driver for this here bunch, you better ride up front with me," he suggested. Retief complied.

As soon as he had clanged the cardboard-upholstered cab door shut, having crowded in beside Retief and the driver, Grundy said in a confidential tone, "How about it, brother? How bad is the war? Where's the Navy? We appreciate the shipment you boys snuck in labelled 'office supplies,' but hand-blasters ain't gonna help much if they decide to stand off and bomb."

"You'll be glad to know that Governor Anderson is on his way home," Retief put in as Grundy ran out of breath. "And his family, too."

"How about Buster, the hired man?" Grundy demanded. "He's the best tech man in the Plantation. Came out here to be a inspector for the outfit installed the SWIFT gear, only the company folded, and he was stranded. Had to take whatever job he could get. He OK too?"

"Buster looked hale and hearty when I saw him last," Retief reassured the sergeant-major. "When the Ree attacked," he went on to inquire, "did they set up a base here, or was it just hit and run?"

"Tried to," Grundy said with satisfaction. "Run, I mean. But we headed 'em off at the draw, and they all committed suicide. Least, they all went rigid and ain't made a move since. Like they was paralyzed, or catatonic or like that. Ain't rotted, so they ain't really dead, I guess."

"The Ree are a practical folk," Retief explained. "If they realize they're trapped, they go into deep hibernation until the coast is clear."

"Well, anyway," the sergeant-major resumed his account, "soon's we took care of that, we got together and decided if the Navy ain't gonna give us coverage, we'd better do something ourselves. That's how come the Planetary Defense Force. Not a real spit-and-polish outfit, but eager to go. You saw that yourself."

"Team Leader Ambassador Sitzfleisch was deeply impressed," Retief assured Grundy.

"I bet we don't get no more static from them Ree," the sergeant-major predicted, "when they get word we're organized and combat-ready."

"You may be right," Retief agreed. "That being the case, it would be a pity to let the troops get stale from lack of action."

"Right! If my boys don't get to loose off a few rounds, now their dander's up, they'll probably start in looting each other."

"I have a solution," Retief said quietly. "Suppose we carry the war to the enemy."

"Whaddaya mean, Retief?" Grundy inquired hesitantly. "How can we do that when they ain't here?"

"Easily," Retief told him. "We can go on the offensive."

"I like it," Grundy said. "By golly, Retief, the boys are gonna love this. 'We,' you said: that mean you're coming, too?"

"I wouldn't miss it," Retief assured the local warlord.

"Course," Grundy said, after a pause, "we don't know what kind of firepower they got, or where they're at."

"I can help you there," Retief advised the sergeant-major. "Do you people maintain contact with McGillicudy's World, Drygulch, Dobe, and the other worlds in the cluster?"

"Sure do, got a nice balance o' payments, too, only we ain't heard from them lately. Last we heard, the worms are harassing them, too, just like us."

"Do you think they'd fight to hold onto their planets?" Retief asked.

"Durn tootin," Grundy responded enthusiastically. "Only they got no more armed forces'n we have—less, since we started the PDF."

"Suppose we rename it the Cluster Defense Force, and find a way to supply arms," Retief suggested. "Would you agree to that?"

"Just what I was thinkin about myself!" Grundy stated: "only I don't know how I could help 'em with arms. We hardly got enough in the sneak shipments for ourselves."

"I have a few ideas," Retief said. "Here's what I have in mind . . ."

Chapter Seven

When the shuffling of feet and clearing of throats had subsided, Team Leader Ambassador Sitzfleisch adjusted his hip-o-matic chair and *harrumph*!ed portentiously, keeping his small, red-rimmed eyes averted from those of his Select Team.

"Gentlemen," he began, "it appears we have acted hastily. It's all very well to counsel appeasement by colonists when one is comfortably situated at Sector HQ. However, now that we, ourselves, and you chaps as well, have been offered as a sacrifice to these blood-thirsty dacoits, and are indeed here in Tip Space surrounded by hordes of the blighters poised to attack with indescribable ferocity at any moment—" he paused for the shudder "—it becomes crystal-clear that some effective move on our part is imperative if we are to survive. Mr. Retief," Sitzfleisch turned to fix his gaze on the latter.

"You will at once prepare my vessel for return to Sector with all deliberate haste."

"That won't be practical, Mr. Ambassador," Retief informed his chief. "I've already agreed to transport the sergeant-major to McGillicudy's World for a conference, after which we'll probably go on to Jawbone and a few other places. It appears the Ree are jamming what little interworld communications capability these frontier planets possess."

"Your agreement was cheeky, I'd say, Mr. Retief," Siztfleisch snapped. "After all, the scheduling of my personal VIP transport is my own prerogative."

"Aside from the fact that *Phoenix* was requisitioned by the CDT for official use only," Retief said, "she was requisitioned from me, presumably on the basis of the idea that a vessel which had once paid a call on Slive would be best qualified to do it again, and I'm still the owner of record. In any case, I've committed the ship to this job, for which the sergeant-major extends his heartfelt gratitude to Your Excellency."

"Umm, well, if you've promised, I suppose . . ."

"Fine, that's settled, then," Retief dismissed the matter. "In the meanwhile," he went on, "you and your troops can keep busy attending to some detail work pending my return." He handed over a list.

"All of you Team members held headquarters jobs of vast importance prior to your selection for the Team," Retief pointed out, "and by some curious oversight possibly connected with an unauthorized visit to Comm Section at Sector, you still retain full powers. My suggestion is that you employ those powers to the fullest to accomplish the chores on my list, and then perhaps Your Excellency's hope of avoiding a dire fate at the tentacles of the Ree inquisitors can be achieved."

"You said 'possibly,' " Sitzfleisch charged. "Not a very compelling term, Mr. Retief. We want your guarantee of success!"

"I'll do my best," Retief replied. "And if you do the same, we may have a chance. That's the best I can do."

"And just what comprises your best, sir?" Sitzfleisch persisted.

"Perhaps," Retief replied reassuringly, "some of us will survive."

2

The planetary leaders assembled in the barn-like Palace of Justice on McGillicudy's World were a rough-hewn lot, Retief observed as they took their places at the battered conference table at the center of the vast, cow-manure-scented, rammed-earth floor.

Sergeant Major Grundy tugged at Retief's sleeve as they seated themselves at the head of the table. "I'll introduce you to the boys," he volunteered. "This here," he indicated the man to his left, "is Chief Heavy Charlie Two-Spears; he's Number One Big Medicine here on McGilli-cudy's." The swarthy, massive-shouldered, big-boned man thrust out an immense, calloused hand adorned with at least one silver-and-turquoise ring on each finger and three on the thumb. The grimy cuff of a blue and yellow mackinaw

reached a point of six inches above his wrist.
Retief shook the hand, as hard as seasoned oak.

"Here you needum help Heavy Charlie go on
Warpath," the Big Medicine said in a bass voice.
"If Great White Father come up with some heavy
artillery for us, spirits say we takum plenty
scalp."

"Sorry, Chief," Retief said. "The Ree are as
hairless as a tube lining."

"OK," Big Charlie said, "Takum whole head
instead, put on spear, decorate doorway."

"Now this here," Grundy broke in, indicating
a square-jawed woman sitting opposite the chief.
"This here is Princess Sally; she's the Matriarch
from Jawbone; got the job by licking all comers,
male, female, or not decided. The princess can
field ten thousand o' the hardest broads that
ever broke a guy's arm which he was only tryna
be friendly." Grundy massaged his left biceps
gently.

Next, Grundy introduced Powerful Pete, an
amazingly tall, cadaverous fellow with pale, near-
sighted eyes and a ferocious mustache, King *pro
tem* from Drygulch. A burly, gnomelike fellow in
the next chair gave Pete a dubious look and
inquired in a voice like a subterranean rockfall,
"How come they call you 'Powerful'?"

"Beats me," Peter replied mildly. He turned
toward the squat man, casually gripped the edge
of his chair-seat with his left hand and lifted the
short man to eye-to-eye level. "Just kind of a
nickname I picked up," he added.

"Speaking of picking up," Grundy put in
bluntly. "Would you leave Commissar Objuck's
chair set on the floor, Pete?"

A burly ex-pug type wearing odds and ends of

well-worn Naval blue polyon was introduced as Cap Josh from Shivaree; his neighbor was a thick-set fellow of remote African extraction, who smiled pleasantly, showing filed teeth, when Grundy presented Chief Umbubu from Moosejaw, and so on along the table. None of the planetary leaders, Reteif noted, was afflicted with an effete appearance or any extraordinary air of over-intellectualization. At last, the ritual of introduction was broken into by a gap-toothed fellow with a bicycle chain wrapped around his fist and a flat leather cap which seemed molded to his flattened skull. "OK, so who's this Mr. Retief, we got to waste all this time telling him our names?" he boomed from the far end of the table.

"Like I told you at first, Nandy," the sergeant-major called back in an impatient tone, "Retief here's our CDT contact, got some great ideas about how we get ourselves organized. Talked about the special arms shipment and all."

A black-bearded ruffian in solid whites with gold buttons responded from beside Nandy:

"If he's the one shipped us the hand-guns labeled hand lotion, he's a all-right guy, right, guys?"

"Wait a minute, Admiral," the Neanderthaloid cut in. "You talk like this slicker thinks he's bossing the show. Nobody bosses Boss Nandy."

"Not unless he qualifies in the traditional fashion, I presume you mean, Boss," a spidery fellow with impressive eyebrows and an elaborately broken nose put in, in an adenoidal voice. "Ha?" he pressed the query.

"Well, Upright," Nandy grunted, rising to reveal a barrel-like torso supported by legs like gnarled parentheses, "I guess that's a legit of a idear, so let's just check out this guy's meat." He started toward the head of the table, exchanging quick handshakes and terse greetings as he went.

"—tell 'em, Boss!"

"—mash this here bum and get back."

"—put on some, ain't you, Nan?"

"—just take a minute . . ."

Watching the approach of the hulking fellow, Grundy whispered to Retief:

"Looks like I got you into a fix here, Retief. But just play it cool; I got a .1mm stashed, and I'll sting him good if he starts to get too rough."

Boss Nandy's rolling gait brought him quickly to confront Retief, who had risen quietly and stood easily, awaiting this challenger's next move. Now, face-to-shirt-front with his intended victim, Nandy hesitated, cocking his lumpy head to peer up at Retief from under brows like the overhang of a rock shelter at Les Eyzies.

"Don't mess with Boss," Grundy advised Retief, *sotto voce*, "he ain't got much restraint, you know."

"He won't be needing any, Sarge," Retief told him.

"Kinda tall, ain't ya, feller?" Nandy commented in his guttural basso, at the same moment making a grab at Retief's arm with a calloused, broken-nailed hand the size of a catcher's mitt.

Retief inobtrusively caught the Boss's forearm, held it immobile, and squeezed. Nandy's lumpy face grew red as he strained silently to free himself from Retief's grip.

"You'd best go back and sit down," Retief

suggested quietly. Nandy nodded, and Retief released the shaggy fellow's arm and started to turn away; just as he raised a hand to his breast pocket, he heard an abrupt scrape of Nandy's shoe-leather, and turned back; as he did, somehow his elbow collided with the Boss's prognathous jaw. Nandy's legs went rubbery, but he caught himself, and stood swaying slightly.

"Oops," Retief said, "did I bump into you, Boss?"

"I never seen them other three guys," Boss mourned. "Anyways, I heard you diplomatic Johnnies was creampuffs. I heard wrong," he added, as the last of the glaze faded from his deep-set, blood-shot eyes.

"May I escort you to your place?" Retief asked. Nandy shook his head. The entire exchange had occurred so swiftly and inobstrusively that no one at the table had observed more than a momentary jostling.

"Maybe you're a all-right guy at that," Nandy muttered. "Keeping it quiet like you done, instead of showing me up in front of the boys."

"We can always put on a show for the boys latter, when your jawbone knits," Retief pointed out pleasantly. Nandy raised his voice to address the table:

"Like I said, Retief here is the operations boss of this caper, and I don't want to hear no complaints."

After a pause, he added. "How about you, Crubby?" The member so addressed was a hulking Mongol type, sweating profusely in a sheepskin vest which exposed biceps like lumpy watermelons, a robber baron from Drywash known to his peers as Tang the Execrable.

Tang gave Nandy a look like a slant-eyed cobra, and grunted. "He's OK with me, pal. Anybody got any objections?" Tang looked slowly along one side of the long table, and back along the other, found only bland smiles and averted eyes.

"Now, let's get on to the details," Sergeant-Major Grundy yelled over the sudden outburst of conversation which followed Tang's challenge. "Retief," he went on, "want to tell 'em about the relief shipments?"

Retief nodded. "Since CDT issue supplies are listed alphabetically," he told his attentive listeners, "errors can occur if the computers hiccup, and skip a space. Hence, orders for hand-lotion are interpreted as 'hand-guns,' flame-retardent paint is adjacent to flame-throwers, and so on. That being the case, I suggest you unpack any recent deliveries of semi-annual requisition items."

"You mean it's all just another bureaucratic snafu?" a mass of bristly black whiskers inquired in a surprisingly melodious tenor voice. "Well," he went on, "no one ever said Stan Spewak was slow on the uptake. Had to disguise what they was doing, so's not to let on they were backing us frontier fellers."

A bull-like man with one arm and a complicated hook arrangement pushed back his chair and rose. "And we ain't gonna let 'em down, are we, boys?" He paused for the roar of approval and the thumping of tankards to subside. "So let's clear port!"

3

Six hours later, with Goldblatt's World looming on the DV screens, which also revealed a swarm of Ree gunboats pacing the intruding Terran convoy, Grundy spoke up:

"So far so good, Retief: I heard you telling that Slive character you'd be on time for your appointment; but I still don't see why they ain't shooting back. Our boys don't rate so good on discipline, I give you that; when they opened up after the word went out to hold fire, I figgered we were in for it. I'm gonna enjoy the court-martial after we land down there."

"That may have to wait," Retief pointed out. At that moment, the ship-to-shore talker tuned to the Ree fleet band cleared its throat and said:

"All right, we want this sucker down all in one piece. Retief is a Special Item, you know. So open up, and let 'em go into descent."

On the screens, the disorderly swarm promptly regrouped into a precise formation through which an open lane remained.

"Shall we steer through there?" Grundy asked, "like they want us to, or do we say to hell with it and scatter 'em?"

The view on the screen immediately made it clear that the question was academic, as the sixty-one units comprising the Cluster expeditionary force spontaneously broke formation and powered through the escorting spates and shoals of Ree gunboats, scattering them like minnows fleeing a carp.

Accepting the *fait accompli*, Grundy, at Retief's nod, used the command talker to order: "All units to independent operational stations; penetrate inner line and rendezvous at previously designated point, which stabilize, over and out."

As the space before them crackled with low-yield missile bursts and the occasional detonation of a gunboat, plus the explosion of at least one CDF irregular, Retief steered *Phoenix* around the most exuberant areas of the fire-fight and entered atmosphere on the far side of the planet, accompanied by a small self-appointed escort, mostly converted luxury boats with hastily installed deck guns, which they used to clear the Ree in a narrow swath.

A squadron of Ree which had followed in his wake peeled off to fly past in salute while he followed a standard approach pattern to the port, taking the same VIP dock to which he had been guided on his previous visit.

Telling Grundy to remain aboard, Retief debarked amid sporadic firing by his escort. This time he ignored the waiting line-cart and commandeered the Ree limousine waiting on standby status.

"Geeze, boss," the startled driver exclaimed, roused from his nap. "What's up? The shooting and all, I mean."

"Nothing much," Retief reassured him as the heavy vehicle started off. "Just a change of administration."

"Cripes! And I never even got to vote," the driver mourned.

"Neither did I." Retief said. "So we cancel out."

With that, the driver whisked him across town to the glossy black tower.

The smartly turned-out sentries stepped forward to bar his way, but Retief waved them aside and leaving the chauffeur to explain matters, made his way unassisted along the narrow passages, now deserted, to Slive's private no-waiting room. The door to the Intimidator's sanc-tum sanctorum was ajar and Retief entered without hesitation. Back of his massive console, Slive looked up as if surprised.

"So, it's you. Precisely on time. Foolish of you. But of course you *are* a fool. Consider: knowing full well the dread fate which awaited you here, you nonetheless came here, uncoerced. Ergo, you are either so incredibly stupid as to have forgotten, or, worse, doubted my promise to terminate your existence—or, even less per-ceptively, failed to realize that simply by staying away, you could have averted that fate. The dullest recruit in the Fleet of Great Ree could have figured that one out. Such appalling lack of wit is, of course, diagnostic of your inade-quate species; thus it is crystal-clear that Des-tiny requires that Great Ree occupy the breeding surfaces otherwise wasted on the support of con-genital inferiors."

"Gosh," Retief said. "I'll bet it's a relief to get that off your chest. Been rehearsing it for a whole month, eh?"

"Hardly," Slive objected. "I but blurted out, *extempore*, the facts as they were clear to one at sight of you. Such dumbness is hardly to be credited."

"I just dropped in to tell you the fun is over, Slive. And your title has been changed: you can call yourself 'IF' now; that's for 'Incompetent Fumbler.' Terra has decided to swat you, IF. Perhaps you noticed a small disturbance in your upper atmosphere starting about an hour ago:

that was my armada squashing your gadflies. Your HQ is now out of business, permanently."

"Absurd!" Slive barked. "Why, at the mere pressing of a button, I can summon my crack first-line squadrons to annihilate any being so lacking in judgment as to infringe Ree sovereignty."

"Try it," Retief suggested. "Be my guest, IF."

Slive pushed a button, then another, without apparent result; then rose and rippled across to the door.

"Freddy!" he yelled, and receiving no reply flung the door wide in time to see the towering figure of Powerful Pete stride into the anteroom, wearing a bandolier across his chest and gripping in one fist a powergun with its hotlight glowing red.

Slive slammed the door. "Drat! Where's Freddy?" he snarled, returning to his chair. "After I elevated the scamp from the ranks to a position of trust! When I need him, he's not to be found!"

"Don't blame Freddy," Retief said mildly. "Sergeant-Major Grundy has him well in hand, no doubt. Now, it's time to get to the substantive portion of today's meeting: I want you to pack up and go home. We'll graciously allow you to do whatever you like in the Western Arm, and I think I can even guarantee you a modest market for glimp eggs. But first, get Snith on the hot-line and chew him out."

"Whatever for?" Slive wanted to know.

"You'll think of something," Retief predicted.

Slive complied silently, and in a moment the Groaci's breathy voice hissed from the talker:

"—here, Slive, to not know just what you have

in mind, but if you'll recall the terms of our *entent cordiale*, to be at once clear to you that this affair of taking back my hostages is not to be borne by proud Groac!"

"Skip all that, Snith," Slive broke in tonelessly. "We got troubles. And speaking *ententes*, what's the idea telling me these Terries would roll up like a rug if I come on like a down-trodden minority? I got this Terry right here in my office now, says he's gonna gimme a break and let me retreat."

"To inquire, my dear Intimidator," Snith came back, "would the name of this rogue Terry, be, ah, 'Retief,' by any fell chance?"

"That's him," Slive confirmed. "You want to talk to him?"

"Lackaday," Snith mourned. "Alas for my dreams of a procuratorship, a haughty Terra humbled, and even a hot tub of sand with the Lady Sith."

"Yeah, that's tough E-pores about the hot sand and all," Slive cut in unfeelingly. "But you better shoo out the rest of the Terry hostages you've been holding out. Don't call me, Mr. Ambassador, I'll call you, if I got anything else to say, which I doubt." He cut the connection.

"Nicely done, Fumbler," Retief congratulated his host. "Now, you had in mind throwing me out that window of yours over there—in fact, you had it installed especially for the purpose, and it would be a pity to let it go to waste. Suppose you go over and look out."

"Never!" Slive barked. "Such devices are suited to the insensitive nervous systems of lower orders which evolved in the tree-tops, dangling by their tails! To a nobleman of Great Ree, the prospect is unthinkable!"

"If just peeking out is that bad, what would you say to sticking your face out and looking straight down?" Retief inquired as he advanced casually toward the former Intimidator.

"Retief! You wouldn't!" Slive hoped aloud.

"It may not be necessary if you cooperate nicely," Retief conceded. It was at that moment that the heavy door burst from its hinges and powerful Pete slammed into the room.

"Oh, hi, Chief," he said casually, switching his blast gun to the yellow-light position. "I guess we got this dump sewed up. Want me to get rid of his Nibs here? Looks like his rank-paint needs retouching."

"Hi, there," Slive caroled. "I'm Incompetent Fumbler Slive, and I was just telling Ambassador Retief about my plans to pull all my troops back into the Western Arm where they belong, and recommend a zero population growth program to the Ultimate."

END

THE SECRET

"Tell His Excellency to get down off that chandelier at once!" Ambassador Smallfrog said in a choked voice. He plucked appealingly at his First Consul's sleeve. "But in a nice way, Ben, of course," he added.

Ben Magnan nodded and rose briskly, glancing up in surprise at the scarlet-robed and gold-braided amoeboid form of the Grotian Minister of Foreign Affairs, which was clinging to the ornate crystal lighting fixture above the table where the three members of the *Corps Diplomatique Terrestrienne*—Ambassador Frederick Smallfrog, First Consul Ben Magnan, and Special Envoy Retief—were plying the Minister with lunch.

"Heavens! How did he get up there?" Ambassador Smallfrog murmured. "He didn't seem the athletic type. Retief!" he whispered sharply to the broad-shouldered Envoy seated to his right. "Do something! But use no force."

Retief rose, studying the manner in which the

short, digitless limbs of the alien were entwined among the branching arms of the chandelier. He drew on his Jorgensen cigar to bring it to a cherry-red glow, gestured the hot end toward the alien's purple-pink hide, and commented distinctly,

"We could, you know, apply heat to the Minister's elbow—or is it a knee?"

The limb immediately contracted, scrambling for new purchase farther from the potential source of discomfort.

Retief waved the cigar closer to the Grotian's nervously quivering form.

The alien retracted his pseudopods and contracted his bulk into a gourd-shaped mass dangling by a single jointless limb.

"Dearie me, Retief," Magnan chirped. "I'm not at all sure Terran-Grote relations are being cemented by your somewhat drastic sign-language. You'd better let well enough alone."

"Factually, I haven't touched him," Retief said. "How else can we get His Excellency's attention to a simple request? He seems pretty much wrapped up in himself."

"Retief, shhh," Magnan interposed hastily, "that comes very close to being a racially biased remark."

"I doubt that His Excellency is in any condition to comprehend it," Retief soothed his senior. "I'm not sure where he keeps his IQ, but by now it must be squeezed pretty flat."

"Retief, hush! He's listening—see how he has his ear cocked."

"Actually," Retief said, studying the puckered organ on the undercurve of the alien's bulk, "I think you'll find that's more of a navel."

"Correct, my boy," said a mellow voice which seemed to issue from the general direction of the dangling diplomat. "Pray excuse my impulsive and probably unconventional act in retreating to this convenient perch. I'll be glad to descend now, since Freddy seems upset about it."

"But, Mr. Minister, we heard you didn't speak Terran," Magnan wailed. "That's why Ambassador Smallfrog has been communicating with you in sign-language all week."

"Indeed? I assumed poor Freddy was merely vocally afflicted."

Magnan resumed his seat and picked at his shrimp cocktail, which consisted of a glass goblet half full of ketchup, with half a dozen extralarge boiled shrimp arranged about its rim. He glanced up and blinked as the alien Minister, once again equipped with various arms and legs, all neatly fitted to the appropriate sleeves and legs of his Terran-tailored satin finery, settled himself in his seat.

"Why, Mr. Minister, you fair gave me a turn," Magnan exclaimed. "I didn't even notice you climbing down. In which connection," he went on, "may I inquire why Your Excellency found it expedient to take up a position on the chandelier just at that time?"

"Doubtless bad protocol on my part, Ben," Foreign Minister D'Ong replied apologetically, "but I was quite upset to find that a number of small innocent creatures had crept into my pudding and expired there. Alas, how melancholy."

He dabbed with his CDT-crested damask napkin at an eye-like organ from which a large tear was welling.

"Pudding?" Magnan echoed. "But dessert hasn't been served yet."

"He means his shrimp cocktail," Retief pointed out quietly.

Magnan glanced at the glass cup half filled with red sauce that had been placed before the alien.

"I don't quite ... er ... understand, Your Excellency," he murmured. "Creatures? Do you suggest that you found ... ah ... some sort of vermin in your cocktail?"

"Not at all, my dear Ben," D'Ong replied. "I simply noted that some charming little fellows, resembling dear relations of my own, had crept over the rim of my cup to steal a bit of the tasty red pudding, and had slipped and fallen in and perished, poor little ones. How too, too sad."

"Retief, he apparently thinks the shrimp are sentient—perhaps household pets," Magnan whispered urgently. "Tell him."

"Better not," Retief said. "It might not be diplomatic to imply that his dear relatives resemble a lower species."

"To be sure, to be sure," Magnan concurred.

"By the way, Mr. Minister," he went on, "how *did* you get down from that chandelier? I was sitting right here, and it seemed as if one second you were up there, and the next you were sitting in your place."

"I got down the same way I went up," the Grotian said, as he stared mournfully at his cocktail cup. "I whoofled, of course."

"How exactly does one whoofle?" Magnan leaned forward to inquire.

"First, one must cinch up the sphlincters nice and tight," D'Ong said mildly. "Then it's essential to take care not to cogitate on trivia—diplomacy, for example. Having thus placed oneself in the proper spiritual frame of reference, one simply concentrates on the desired destination and—whoofles."

"Gosh, sir, it sounds easy," Magnan gushed. "Retief, just think of staff meetings—when you think you can't stand it another second—just tighten up the old sphlincters, think of a comfy park bench—and you're off!"

"Sounds OK," Retief agreed.

"I can't wait to try," Magnan said.

"You'll never whoofle while thinking of staff meetings," D'Ong sighed. "And beware of impulsive inclinations to twaffle with unsettling matters on the agenda."

"Twaffle, sir? What's that?" Magnan cried.

A pink-veined crustacean gave a leap from the rim of the Minister's cocktail glass and flew across the white-linened table. Soon the other crustaceans in the glass were twitching and leaping among the crystal and silver.

"What the devil's *this*?" the voice of Ambassador Smallfrog boomed out abruptly.

"Gracious, that's his 4-c Bellow," Magnan whispered, looking anxiously at Retief.

"Wrong, Ben!" Smallfrog roared. "That was my 4-z, and I've heard tell I have one of the finest 4-z's in the corps! Now," he proceeded more calmly, "what's the meaning of this?"

He held up a wiggling fugitive from the cocktail glass.

At that moment, Magnan yelped and groped in his lap. He held up a duplicate of the creature the Ambassador was displaying. "It just sort of sprang at me," he blurted.

"Serving live shrimp at table!" Smallfrog boomed. "Possibly the chef's idea of a capital jape."

"Oh, hardly, Mr. Ambassador," Retief said. "The shrimp are processed and deep-frozen before being exported from Terra. Obviously the Minister—in understandable shock at a specious resemblance—is merely twaffling."

"I appreciate your sympathy, Retief," D'Ong said. He indicated Retief's untouched shrimp cocktail. "You say that the resemblance is specious. Do you mean that the creatures in our puddings—?"

"The shrimp, as far as we know, are not sentient beings," Retief explained. "They are, to the contrary, a source of delicious food."

He grasped the tail of a shrimp in his glass, dipped the shrimp into the sauce, and took a savoring bite.

"Hm. It does look good," D'Ong acknowledged. "Perhaps a teensy morsel—"

"Take the Ambassador's portion," Retief offered, sliding the glass across the tablecloth. "Protocol forbade him to start eating before you did."

As Retief and D'Ong dipped and munched the tasty shrimp, Ambassador Smallfrog and Magnan drew their chairs together at the opposite corner of the table.

"Are you thinking what I'm thinking?" the Ambassador muttered. "When D'Ong whoofles, he—ah—"

"Teleports?" Magnan ventured.

"And when he twaffles, he—ah—"

"Is applying telekinesis?"

"Exactly, Magnan," the Ambassador said. "You

have achieved the difficult maneuver of Deduction Under Pressure, Reg. K72. Congratulations. Extrasensory skills!" he whispered further, with rapture. "Terra *must* secure the Most Favored Planet treaty with Grote. We never suspected they had such—"

He broke off, and his face became anxious. "Do you suppose those five-eyed, weak-kneed, deceptive little scoundrels, the Groaci, are aware of this extraordinary talent? Is that why their Ambassador Shiss is pushing D'Ong for a Groaci treaty?"

D'Ong, having ingested the Ambassador's shrimp, asked Retief curiously, "Why have your superior officers withdrawn from us into that mumbling?"

"Terran higher echelon diplomats can't eat and think at the same time," Retief explained.

"How similar the species are!" D'Ong agreed.

The shrimp was succeeded by *boeuf aux champignons* and raspberry trifle. As the waiter cleared the table, Ambassador Smallfrog moved his chair back to its original position, and began.

"To resume our discussion of the mutually beneficial interplanet trade tready, Minister D'Ong, is there any little thing you'd like to request from Terra?"

"Right now, Freddy, old boy," D'Ong said, "I could use a quaff of that magic drink from ancient Terra."

The three Terran diplomats exchanged questioning glances. Ambassador Smallfrog suggested, "A Bacchus black? A daquiri sting? A nip of brandy?"

"If I might request a pot of hot water," D'Ong

said diffidently. "I think I can offer a demonstration."

Magnan called back the waiter and issued the order.

"Hot water? Hmph," Smallfrog snorted. "Since when do diplomats imbibe water, hot or otherwise?"

"Gracious," Magnan murmured behind his hand to Retief. "All this fuss over what was intended to be a cosy little tête-a-tête, to make some mileage with the Grotes before that sneaky little Ambassador Shiss has a chance to start toadying up to poor dear D'Ong. And Ambassador Smallfrog is never at his best when faced with the unexpected. I suggest we slip out and keep an eye on the Groaci Embassy. Perhaps Shiss is behind the foolish rumor that Terrans can do magic with hot water."

Retief gestured him to silence.

The waiter loomed, pot in hand.

"Just put it down, my man," the Grotian Foreign Minister said quietly. "Leave four cups."

The waiter obeyed and withdrew.

Magnan lifted the lid of the handsome Yalcan teapot and peeked inside. He sniffed. "Hot water, just as His Excellency specified."

"So. Hot water to top off a lunch of jumping shrimp and puzzling issues," Smallfrog remarked with false joviality.

"Ah, sir, as to the rather unusual events—" Magnan started, only to be cut off by a peremptory Ambassadorial gesture.

"Never explain, Magnan. Unless I order you to, of course. With your friends it isn't necessary, and with your superiors it doesn't work. An interesting entry in your form 163-9, Ben—'this officer has an unusual sense of humor.' Perhaps it won't seem *too* bad when the Promotion Board is mulling it over. Shall I pour?" He lifted the pot. "Hot water, Mr. Minister?"

D'Ong eagerly offered his cup for filling. He groped in a satin pocket with a seven-fingered hand and brought out a small filter-paper packet, limp and stained, with a short length of string attached. Calmly he dipped it into his cup, the contents of which immediately turned a rich amber.

He withdrew the bag and with a courteous nod, dunked it into Smallfrog's cup. Then in turn, into Magnan's and Retief's, dyeing each the same deep color.

Smallfrog hesitated, lifted his cup, and sipped carefully. A somewhat forced smile contorted his meaty features. "Gad, sir," he said. "Orange Pekoe, my—er—favorite. Ann Page, too, if my memory serves me right."

Magnan tried his. It was tea, no doubt of it.

"A delightful brew," D'Ong said. "A souvenir of my great-aunt R'Oot's visit to Terra a few centuries ago. I keep it for sentimental reasons. And as a matter of taste, of course.

"Poor auntie passed away last week," D'Ong went on, "leaving me a few hundred million in gold squiggs and green stamps. Decent old girl. I remember when she used to dandle me on a knee she extruded just for the purpose. Alas, I won't be seeing her again, unless she decides to furfle—and I don't see why she should."

"To—to furfle? Goodness, D'Ong," Magnan asked, "how does one furfle?"

"First, one has to be dead. Quite dead, you

understand, Ben. Indisputably beyond the quaffling stage."

"And quaffling is—?"

"Very useful." D'Ong's glance went to the tea
bag he had laid neatly in his saucer. "But let us
not linger over poor Auntie. Freddy has asked
what would sweeten the treaty deal. How about
a gift of a magic drink pouch for every Grotian
household?"

"Ah—well—one moment, Minister," Ambassador Smallfrog said, drawing back to consult with
Magnan. "Ben, do we have—?"

"Not at the Embassy, sir," Magnan said apologetically. "It's true that traditional ethnic groups
and historical societies cultivate the use of tea-
bags, but—" He paused. "The Ladies Auxiliary
might possibly—"

"Magnan!" Smallfrog reproved in a low voice.
"Would you imply that His Excellency has taste
in common with the Ladies Auxiliary?"

"He may hold ladies in high esteem, sir. Not
that I'm saying you don't, sir. I mean—"

"You certainly wouldn't accuse a superior of
undiplomatic prejudice, I hope," Smallfrog
muttered.

D'Ong drained his cup, wrapped the tea-bag
neatly in a small scarf, put it among the folds of
his scarlet robe, and rose from his chair.

"A pleasurable lunch, Retief," he said, "but
now poor Freddy and Ben have withdrawn to
think again, and I'm late for my appointment
with Groaci Ambassador Shiss."

Retief rose, also. "I'll escort you to the door,
Your Excellency. Don't let the Groaci impose on
your good nature. On behalf of Terra I can assure you the tea is in the bag."

Ambassador Smallfrog and his First Consul struggled hastily to their feet and bade adieu to the Foreign Minister, who left the room under Retief's escort.

"I don't need to tell you, Ben, this is a critical moment for Terry-Grote relations," Smallfrog said, dropping into his chair. "Lying as it does, squarely athwart the lanes of expansion of Terran Manifest Destiny, Grote—though a trivial world in itself—can pose an awkward problem should Groaci influence become dominant here.

"But before expanding on that theme," he went on, "I must ask you, Ben, if you saw what *I* saw a moment ago. Or am I hallucinating?"

"Hallucinating, sir? Oh, hardly that, sir. All you've had to drink is a cup of hot water."

"Skip all that, Ben. Did you see what that fellow *did*? Brewed four cups of hearty tea from a single used tea-bag. By gad, sir, *there's* a trick that will cinch the Deputy Under-Secretary slot for me if I can report how it's done. That is to say, an apparent suspension of natural law such as this must surely be looked into!"

"Right," Magnan agreed suavely, "and I imagine it would be a feather in the cap of the officer who is able to bring the information to you. I'd better hurry off at once."

"Sit down, Magnan. I fear you don't fully appreciate the gravity of the matter I've entrusted to you. See to it you don't let the secret of the tea-bag slip from our grasp. Procure tea-bags and see what D'Ong does to them. If you succeed in this mission, tea-bagwise, there may be laurels in the offing for you yet."

"But, sir, procuring the tea-bags will take

time. We must foil the Groaci Shiss right now.
Do you suppose—?" Magnan hesitated.

"Never start a speculation you can't finish,"
Smallfrog advised, "especially to a superior. Well,
what do I suppose?"

"Would D'Ong accept coffee cachets as a temporary substitute? Until we obtain the tea, I
mean."

Smallfrog frowned. "Regular or decaf?"

"I could procure a sample of each from the
kitchen, sir, and intercept D'Ong before he
reaches the Groaci Embassy."

As Magnan hastened to the kitchen, Retief
returned from the front door. Ambassador Smallfrog said, "Retief! Has D'Ong departed already?
We must have him back!"

"Shall I go after him, Ambassador?" Retief
asked.

"Yes—that is, no, Retief. Magnan is earning
merit points. Ah, here he is," he added, as
Magnan returned. "Regular and decaf?"

"One in each pocket, sir!"

Magnan hurried through the Embassy hall
and emerged on the front terrace. The broad
avenue, curving away under the shady boughs
of the imported heo trees, was deserted.

The big Marine sergeant at the Embassy gate
snapped to present arms.

"At ease, Jim," Magnan said testily. "Didn't
Foreign Minister D'Ong go out just now?"

"Yessir—and nossir. Funny thing." Jim grounded his power gun, abandoning the attempt to
maintain the Position of a Soldier. "For a second I didn't get it. Saw him come ankling down
the steps and along the walk. D'Ong's a nice
guy—usually stops to chat a minute, you know—

but this time he did some kind of tricky side-step and jumped right out of sight.

"I figured maybe he'd wobbled into the bushes. These local pseudopods sometimes get unsteady on their extrusions. But I checked, and nope—nobody there except Mr. Prutty from the Econ Section smooching his neat little secretary, Miss Rumpwell. That's some duty, Mr. Magnan," he said indignantly. "While I've got to stand watch here, four-on, eight-off, this clown gets ten times my pay for keeping the help harmoniously adjusted to life at a hardship post—leastways that's what he told me. I invited Miss Rumpwell out three times and got a chill-off that'd give an Eskimo frost-bite, and then she goes for that crummy civilian—no offense, Mr. Magnan."

"None taken, Jimmy. But to return to Foreign Minister D'Ong—"

"It was screwy, Mr. Magnan. He sort of emerged, like. And the next I saw of him he was outside the gate, moving right along. But I swear he never passed me."

"Perhaps you dozed for a moment."

"Not me, Mr. Magnan. It don't add up. But come to think of it, I saw that crummy Groaci Fith hanging around across the street. Had a little pink parasol, made him look like a five-eyed Madam Butterfly. Maybe he had something to do with it, huh?"

"Probably routine surveillance. I suggest you forget the matter, Sergeant," Magnan said stiffly. "No point in blowing it up into an interplanetary issue."

"OK, but I'm gonna keep a sharp eye on the next local comes in here."

"Quite right, my boy. Now I must be off. By

the way, if Foreign Minister D'Ong should reappear in the next few minutes, just detain him in a casual way until I get back."

"I'll see what I can do. You don't want me to arrest anybody, I guess."

"Gracious, no, Jimmy. Arrest? Whatever for?"

Magnan walked through the great wrought-iron gate and hurried away along Embassy Row. He went past the high board fence which concealed the deep mut-pit housing the Yulcan Consulate General, the placid pond under which lay the Rockamorran Legation, and the haughty, classic facade of the Sulinorean Mission to Grote.

Next, there was a broad vacant lot with a "For Loan" sign almost invisible among the pitzle-weeds, then the low, unprepossessing structure of the Jaque Chancery. Beyond it, impregnable behind a high stone wall, the Groaci Embassy resembled an Assyrian maximum-security prison as visualized by the Galactic Teleview Theater.

Magnan slowed to a casual saunter, veering close to the plate-steel gate to dart a quick glance through the 4-inch keyhole.

"Hi, Ben," a breathy voice called from behind the gate. "Anything I can do for you?"

Magnan executed a two-step, registering astonishment.

"That 709 Back-and-Fill of yours needs work, Ben," the same faint voice commented. "What brings a Terry First Secretary, on foot already, to the gates of the Groacian Mission on such a warm afternoon?"

"Just passing by, Fith," Magnan replied in a tone of Casual Indifference.

"Don't waste a 301 Indifference on me, Ben,"

Fith suggested. "If you expect to get a glimpse of nefarious doings right out in the driveway, forget it. Ambassador Shiss is too old a campaigner. He's got a special nefarious-stuff room for that kind of caper. Not that us peace-loving Groaci go in for skullduggery, you understand."

"Of course, of course, Fith. It couldn't have been you the Marine Guard saw lurking outside our Embassy. But what in the world are you, a company grade officer, doing pulling two-on and four-off?"

"Well, Ben, frankly, His Excellency has had it in for me ever since he caught me climbing into a tub of hot sand with the Lady Trish last Wednesday, when the old goof was supposed to be safely off watching a game of flat-ball over at the Inertian Consulate.

"All perfectly innocent, of course," he added. "Her ladyship just asked me to check the temperature of her bath for her, to be sure she wouldn't get any damage to the ziff-nodes from that high, infra-red radiation, you know."

"But, of course, Fith—we're both beings-of-the-world," Magnan said tolerantly. "Er—by the way—Foreign Minister D'Ong arrived here a few minutes ago, didn't he?"

"Nope. I'm keeping four or five eyes out for him. Supposed to be here any time now. You don't happen to see an official limousine coming with the poor boob in it, do you?"

"No," said a soft voice behind Magnan, "but here's the poor boob in person."

Magnan whirled around. D'Ong stood at his elbow, robed now in green satin and silver braid, and with a serene expression on his rather lumpy features.

"Your Excellency!" Magnan gasped. "I wondered where you—I mean, obviously you went home to change your attire."

"New appointment, fresh robe. You Terrans are so drab," D'Ong said critically.

"We weren't always—drab, I mean," Magnan apologized. "In ancient times we wore cloaks and doublets and garters and such. Nowadays the fancy robes are worn by the Ladies Auxiliary—no offense, Excellency."

"None taken. More power to the girls," D'Ong said cheerily. "But what are you doing here, Ben? I hardly expected the pleasure so soon."

"Well, that's diplomacy, Your Excellency. One keeps running into the same people—like Fith here—just beyond the gate, that is," Magnan said in a warning tone. "Fith was Consular Officer at Slunch when I was a mere Third Secretary. And then later, at Furtheron, we both served on the Chumship Team, arbitrating the Civil War. That's where I got this gash on the arm."

Magnan turned his cuff to expose a crescent-shaped scar.

"Nasty," D'Ong commented. "Got that in the War, did you?"

"No, at the conference table. Between us, Mr. Minister," he continued in a whisper, "while Fith, like all Groaci, can be a charming fellow, he has a tendency to bite when crossed."

"Well, enough of nostalgia for the moment, Ben," D'Ong said. "I mustn't keep Ambassador Shiss waiting. Until tomorrow at the jelly-flower judging, then?"

"Ah—wait—Mr. Minister—"

"Just call me D'Ong," the Grotian said affably.

"All that 'Mr. Minister' jazz gives me a swift pain in the zop-slot."

"Sure, er, D'Ong," Magnan agreed. "Why don't you and I sneak off for a couple quick cups of tea, and let old Shiss stew in his own juice?"

"I couldn't think of it, Ben. One doesn't stand up a fellow-being, no matter how tiresome he may be."

"Yes, but frankly, D'Ong, I have a feeling Shiss is up to no good. On the other hand, if I could speak to you for a moment, I could explain about a real treaty-sweetener as advantageous as your auntie's tea bag."

"Why couldn't you have explained it at the lunch, instead of mumbling away to Freddy?"

"Well, we only thought of it—"

"Halt! What scheming Terry trick are you up to, Magnan?" Fith demanded through the key-hole. "How fortunate I alerted the guard at your unheralded approach!"

There was a sudden outburst of breathy Groaci shouting from beyond the wall. A bolt screeched at being withdrawn, and the massive gate swung back.

A platoon of Groaci peace-keepers in flaring red helmets and chrome-plated greaves with red and green studs emerged in a ragged column of twos.

"To surround the soft ones instanter!" a non-com whispered in harsh Groaci.

The troops at once formed a lopsided circle around Magnan and D'Ong, power guns at the ready.

"Here, here, I protest!" Magnan cried. "Captain Fith!" He fixed the officer with an Indignant

Stare (491-a) "You're making a serious blunder! Call off your boys at once!"

"You know how it is, Ben," Fith said in his accentless Terran. "Got to keep on top of the situation. This puts me one-up. No hard feelings."

"*Au contraire*, I shall have very hard feelings indeed unless Minister D'Ong and I receive an immediate apology."

A hoarse Groaci voice called from beyond the wall, "To do your duty at once, Captain Fith—ah, Major Fith, that is, as soon as you have him bound hand, foot, and incidental members, and deposited in the torture cage."

"You see how it is, Ben," Fith said sadly. "Ambassador Shiss is taking a personal interest in the caper." He turned to address the corporal of the guard. "You heard His Excellency. Tie him up! Be quick about it, nest-fouling litter-mate of drones!"

The corporal paused to jot a note on his cuff, then laid hands on D'Ong.

"Not the Foreign Minister—the Terry!" Brevet-Major Fith snapped. "Escort the Minister to his appointment in His Excellency's office."

"Steady, Ben," D'Ong murmured. "I'm sure there'll eventually be a nice note of apology from the Groaci Foreign Office. But—"

He broke off as a pair of Groaci peace-keepers seized him and hustled him up the broad steps and into the Embassy.

Fith's sticky fingers were exploring Magnan's jacket pocket. They came out with the small packets of coffee.

"What's this, Ben?" he asked. "A new product of Terran know-how?"

"An old beverage, Fith," Magnan said, struggling against his captors. "Not worth drinking, really."

"Poison? Not smart of you, Ben, seeking to poison Shiss and D'Ong and thus delay the signing of the Groaci treaty." Fith tossed the packets outside the gate.

The penetrating voice of Ambassador Shiss called from beyond the wall, "Let's get this show on the road—Lieutenant."

Fith leaped as if prodded by an electrospur.

"There goes the old promotion," he mourned. "Drag him in, boys," he added to his troops.

Four Groaci lifted Magnan bodily and staggered off with him, to the ground-level dungeon door. The massive Embassy gates clanged shut.

Meanwhile Ambassador Smallfrog and Retief had adjoured to the No. 2 Reception Salon, and were refreshing themselves with a flagon of Bacchus black.

"By gad, Retief," Smallfrog declared, placing his Toby mug on the table with emphasis, "a permatized tea bag ought to get me the Undersecretary-ship on Kreel, if not better. Did I tell you how I bested the Kreels during my Third Assistant days under old Charlie Gumlip? Well, my boy—"

An hour later he paused in his narrative and remarked, "Ben is taking rather long to convince the Foreign Minister."

"If he, indeed, was able to reach him, Mr. Ambassador," Retief pointed out.

"Goodness gracious, Retief, Ben had only to step down the avenue to the Groaci Embassy," Smallfrog protested.

"Exactly. The Groaci Embassy," Retief said quietly.

"Hmph," Smallfrog snorted. "You'd best run down there, Retief, and find out what has happened. No telling what *faux pas* Ben has committed, in his eagerness to win merit points."

"I agree there's no telling, with the Groaci," Retief said.

He rose, sauntered down the hall, and out the front door. He paused on the terrace, enjoying the cedar-scented evening air. Grote's large pale-blue sun was near the horizon, and the shadows were dense beneath the heo trees.

At the Embassy gate, the Marine guard came to attention. Retief nodded, " 'Evening, Jimmy. Have you seen Mr. Magnan? Which way did he go?"

"He was headed for the Groaci Embassy, looking for D'Ong. Funny, the way D'Ong slipped right past me. I hope I didn't goof, letting him get away with it."

"Not at all, Jim. I'm going to stroll that way and see what there is to be seen."

Retief ambled along the shaded walk. Nearing the Groaci Embassy, he studied the high, grayish-ocher walls, topped with corroded spikes. At the gate he paused, and stooped to pick up a flattened coffee packet from among the trampled leaves. He studied it thoughtfully, dropped it again, and approached the peep-hole in the massive metal gate. He rapped on it twice, and it slid back to reveal a cluster of eye-stalks in plain G. I. eyeshields.

" 'Evening, Captain Fith," Retief said. "Where's Magnan?"

"To imply that I, a peace-loving Groacian

national, doing his simple duty, am aware of the comings and goings of Terry First Secretaries?" a breathy voice replied, then added in accent-free Terran, "Shucks, Retief, I just came on duty. You had an idea Ben was here?"

"Never mind, Fith. I just thought maybe we could skip the formalities and get right to the point. If you boys are holding Mr. Magnan in your compound against his will, we'll have to call out a squadron of Peace Enforcers to make it clear, one more time, that you can't get away with it."

"Curious fancy on your part, Retief. Why would we Groaci be interested in detaining a mere Terry?"

"Skip it. Where's D'Ong?"

"You refer to the feckless local Foreign Minister? He is, I believe, closeted at this moment with His Excellency, Ambassador Shiss, discussing means of enhancing Grote-Groaci relations—not that it's any of your business."

"Better check your manual, Fith. This is too early in the treaty negotiations to start using your Tentative Insolence, 931-y. Stick to a 21-b Cautious Impertinence for the present, or old Shiss will have you on the carpet for impairing Terry-Groaci relations."

"Mmm. To withdraw now, Retief, to see to my routine duties, such as inspecting my sluggards unaware, gold-bricking in the therapeutic sand-pit, instead of cleaning their power guns as instructed."

He slammed the peep-hole cover.

Retief went along to the corner and glanced down the narrow avenue that ran along the north side of the Groaci Embassy compound.

The leaf-strewn sidewalks were deserted. A lone Yillian delivery van was slumped at the curb near the rear gate to the compound. Retief noted that it bore a legend painted in Yillian characters that resembled the word 'egg-nog,' indicating that it was the Yillian Consul-General's formal garbage truck. He noted as he passed it that it listed heavily to starboard. A sour odor of fermenting refuse hung over the grubby vehicle.

Retief snorted and tried the rear gate. It was solidly locked. He stepped back and kicked it at lock height. There was a metallic tinkle and the gate swung ajar. At once, the snout of a Groaci power gun poled through the opening, then withdrew.

There was the creak of a rusted chassis sagging on broken shock absorbers. Retief turned to see a heavy, gray-skinned Yill ponderously emerging from the side door of the garbage truck.

"You Terries got an eye on this dump, too, huh?" the Yill said in a glutinous voice. "Some funny stuff going on around here. One of our boys came over to deliver a birthday stew to His Groacian Excellency and never came out again. Swell glimp-egg stew it was, too, aged six months, just ripe enough but not *too* ripe, you know?"

"How long ago was that, F'Lin-lin?" Retief inquired.

"About two weeks, come sundown. Hey, I just noticed—they goofed and left the gate open."

"Careful," Retief cautioned as the Yill approached the gate. "There's a power gun just inside."

"Sure, I know all that stuff," F'Lin-lin said

carelessly. Reaching the gate, he thrust it open and instantly stepped back and flattened himself against the fence beside it. When the gun muzzle poked out, F'Lin-lin grabbed it and held on.

"Watch it," Retief advised. "If he's on the ball, he'll set it at low beam and maximum choke, and it'll be red-hot in a few seconds."

The Yill grunted and released the gun, which at once withdrew, while F'Lin-lin blew on his palm and muttered.

Retief took up a position against the fence on the hinge side of the gate. After a few seconds a finger-like member poked out hesitantly. Retief caught the six-inch stalk tipped by a bulbous blue ocular, and held it gently but firmly as it twitched.

"Nice going, Retief," F'Lin-lin said. "I always wanted to pull one of their wiggly eyeballs out by the roots. Interesting to see how much stress it'll take to do it."

"To see anything, Quilf?" a wispy voice called from beyond the gate.

"Not precisely to *see* anything, Whiff, but there's something rather curious going on. It got completely dark all of a sudden, and—well, better give me a hand. No!" came a gasp. "Not to try to drag me back. I have my eye fixed on something interesting."

At once a second Groaci thrust out his head, all five eyes erect and alert. Retief released Quilf's eye-stalk, grabbed Whiff by the neck and assisted him out.

The Groaci made a vengeful swipe with a heavy knout, missing Retief's head by an inch. Retief caught the weapon and wrenched it from

the other's grasp. He broke it in two and returned the handle-end to his assailant.

"Be nice, Whiff, and I won't tell anybody what
happened. You can explain that you broke it
over my skull."

"To be sure, Terry. A consummation devoutly
to be wished. Why are you skulking here?"

"Where's Magnan?"

"Where you, too, will end up, vile miscreant—
on the interrogation rack."

Retief lifted the business end of the knout.
"We agreed, I think, that you and Quilf have no
further interest in my fate."

The two Graoci shrank aside and scuttled
away.

"Shall we?" Retief inquired of the Yill and
indicated the abandoned gate, now swinging
wide to reveal a cobbled court lined with stalls
in which poorly maintained Groaci ground-cars
were parked.

A lone Groaci in a ribbed hip-cloak leaned
casually against the wall by the dark, dungeon
archway, fingering a six-foot pike. He came to a
slack-twisted position of attention as Retief
approached, covering the agitated twitching of
his eye-stalks by pretending to adjust his top-
three-grader eye-shields.

"What's up, Retief?" he wheezed. "I guess it
was you that spooked Private Quilf."

"Yes, Sergeant. I caught his eye and gave him
the nod. Obliging fellow."

"Left the gate open, too," the sergeant said.
"Quilf is overdue for a few hours on pots and
pans, I guess. By the way, why are you violating
the sacred precincts of the Groacian Embassy?"

"Just dropped by to remind Mr. Magnan of a staff meeting. Which way?"

"I'd like to escort you, but I can't leave my post. I see that Yill no-good F'Lin-lin, hanging around there."

"What's your name, Sergeant?" Retief asked.

"Yish," the Groaci replied.

"It seems to me I remember you from somewhere," Retief said. "Squeem, perhaps?"

"I was there when the dam let go," Yish conceded. "I lost my stamp collection in the flood—and I've never been convinced you weren't behind the collapse of our lovely new dam."

"Several hundred yards of it," Retief agreed.

"To have a personal score to settle, wise guy!"

The Groaci jabbed suddenly at Retief with his broad-headed pike. Retief moved aside. The sharp point slid past him and nicked the door frame. Yish withdrew it and jabbed again.

"To stand still, miscreant!" he hissed.

The point lodged firmly in the hard wood. Grasping for the shaft, Retief was overpowered by the stench of prime Yill garbage as F'Lin-lin jumped forward and jerked the point free.

The off-balance Groaci relinquished his hold on the pike and sat down suddenly. F'Lin-lin reversed the weapon and aimed it at Yish's throat sac.

"What was that crack about a Yill no-good?" he growled.

"To disregard," panted the Groaci weakly. "To assure the generous Yill the remark referred to somebody else."

"Thanks, F'Lin-lin," Retief said. "Keep him here, will you? And, Yish," he added to the Groacian, huddled in his crumpled hip-cloak, several umbrella-like ribs of which were now hopelessly buckled, "stay quiet, before you lose any more face than you have to."

The dungeon door was not barred. Retief opened it, walked noiselessly along a dim, stone-flagged passageway, and came to a downward spiralling staircase. He heard anguished cries from the lower region, and tiptoed down the stone stairs. As he descended, the cries became clearer.

"Nith, you leather-brained rascal," Magnan was shouting. "I demand to see the Ambassador at once!"

Retief cautiously stepped into the lower passageway and peered into the cell from which the demand was echoing. He saw Magnan strapped to a conversation rack. A leather-aproned executioner confronted him.

"No use being a sorehead about it, Ben," Nith was saying. "Actually, you surprise me. I expected you, as one who has survived staking-out in the sulphur pits of Yush, to stand up to a routine interview in more Spartan fashion."

"It's the indignity of the thing," Magnan explained in a sulky tone. "After all, this wicker-work strait-jacket hardly allows a person to breathe."

"Just spill a few official secrets, Ben, and you'll be breathing in a trice. By the way, what's a trice?"

"It's what you'll be in jail in, as soon as my chief learns of my situation."

"Old Freddy? Forget it, Ben. Now, how about starting with whatever you figured you'd accomplish, snooping around here today."

"I was hardly 'snooping' as you so insolently

put it, my dear Nith. I was innocently waiting for Foreign Minister D'Ong, whom I wished to consult most urgently."

"Ah, yes, the insidious D'Ong. We've had our eye-stalks zeroed in on that fellow for some time. Not quite the standard bureaucrat."

"Nonsense. It's just that he whoofles easily."

"Grotian semantics will not save you," Nith warned, finishing off a package of smoked gribble-grubs. "You've remained adamant under the torments of the toe-tickler and the Tantalizing Tasties, and even endured a half hour of tape-recorded staff meetings—in an alien tongue, yet.

"But you'll not so easily shrug off the upcoming torture. In the very next cell is a cinema projector, a screen, and a full program of old Nelson Eddy movies. Thereafter, a broken man, you'll be only too happy to sob out your secrets."

"Oh, not Nelson Eddy!" Magnan cried. "Spare me that!"

"Nelson Eddy *and* the Andrews Sisters," said Nith remorselessly.

He turned to open an inner door. Retief poised to spring to Magnan's aid—then froze as Nith swung back to confront Magnan.

"The projector and the screen are gone. Vile Terry, who has been here?"

"Why, only yourself," said Magnan. "You went into that room after you first tied me up."

"Hm, so I did, making sure the Roy Rogers movies were in stock," Nith said. "The disappearances are a mystery. I must discuss them with Shiss."

He started for the stairs. Retief hid in an adjacent cell until he was gone. When the Groaci's footsteps had faded away, Retief entered the torture chamber.

"Retief!" cried Magnan. "Save me! To be forced to view a Roy Rogers movie is a fate worse than death!"

Retief examined the harness restraining Magnan, then jerked the straps loose. The wickerwork fell away. Magnan stepped down from the conversation rack with a sigh of relief.

"Let's get out of here while the getting's good," he said. "Two merit points are not commensurate with the danger of the job."

"We can't leave before we've seen Minister D'Ong," Retief objected. "D'Ong may also be in danger."

"But he *did* have an appointment with Ambassador Shiss, you know. And I'm sure," Magnan said nervously, "that it's very bad protocol to conduct unauthorized searches of other embassies. I feel strongly that we must report to Smallfrog before taking any action."

"I certainly won't keep you from reporting," Retief said. "Go up the stairs and follow the passageway to the outer door. A Yill named F'Lin-lin is rendering Sergeant Yish a spent force."

"Aren't you coming, too?"

"No. I'll look around down here for a stairway to the main part of the embassy."

"Now, Retief," Magnan said severely, "as your immediate supervisor, I must caution you to do nothing rash."

"Actually, Mr. Magnan, I haven't yet thought up anything rash to do."

"Excellent. Perhaps you're learning restraint at last."

"I guess it had to happen. But why should we be any more restrained than we have to? After an hour in a Groaci conversation frame, I should think you'd like being unrestrained."

"Ah, yes. To be sure, Retief. Nith stepped a bit over the line restraint-wise in trussing a Terran First Secretary and Consul in that fashion. Still, he merely hinted at the other torments he had planned. He stopped short of screening them."

"So, inasmuch as you have Nith's dossier well in hand, it seems logical for me to tackle his boss."

"Umm. I trust you employ the term 'tackle' figuratively."

"I don't expect to have too much trouble with the old boy. After all, he's a career bureaucrat, too."

"Retief, need I caution you not to rely on any fellow-feeling from that sneaky, five-eyed little devil?"

"Nope."

"I thought not. Just employ standard diplomatic techniques. Shiss is enough of an old campaigner to yield gracefully to a proper approach."

"I assume from that you'd be against my braiding his eyes together, or pinching his air bladder shut."

"Correct. Go in there like a true bureaucrat, Retief. Let him know we've got the dirt on him, though, of course, we wouldn't dream of giving it to the media—as long as he confides in us his object in a Grotian treaty."

Leaving these words of advice, Magnan hurried up the stairs.

Retief continued along the low-ceilinged passage, past barred cell doors and what looked like large fish bones heaped on the stone-slab floors, among rusted chains. Ahead a dim light burned, illuminating a wider staircase. He followed it upwards to a vast portal. He poked at it with a finger. It swung easily back, revealing a gloomy and cavernous hall, dim-lit by tapers on tall wrought-iron standards.

A narrow spiral stair led upward at the far side of the great hall. Aside from a number of impervious-looking doors set in deep recesses, the surrounding walls were featureless stone.

As Retief paused at the top of the staircase, peering beyond the portal, a door opened along the hall. Five familiar eye-stalks bent in his direction.

"To stop there, snooping Retief!" Fith croaked, dashing toward him. "To arrest you on the spot."

"For what?"

"Trespassing, invasion, violation of Groaci sovereignty—"

"Hold it, Fith. You make me sound like an enemy planet."

"To rue the day you intruded here, Terry evil-doer!"

"Where's Foreign Minister D'Ong?"

"That, Retief, is a secret of the Groaci state. No more questions. To descend to the dungeons."

"I'd rather not. I just came from there."

Fith made an odd motion of several eyes. A black-clad Groaci stepped from the shadows behind the portal, delicately fingering a long stiletto.

"Hired muscle," Fith said. "My apologies, Retief, but that's the way it has to be."

The hit-man edged toward Retief, who stepped

forward to meet him. As the Groaci went into a menacing crouch, Retief caught him firmly by the neck, up-ended him, producing a rain of coins and other small objects, shook him once, and tossed him down the staircase. He tumbled with increasing momentum, but it seemed a long time before a heavy *crump!* announced his arrival below.

Retief picked up the knife his would-be assassin had dropped. "Cheap goods," he commented. "If that's hired muscle, I wonder what the free stuff is like."

"Well, you know how it is, Retief. You can't hardly get good help these days."

"I heard that," a resentful voice wheezed from below. "Some loyalty. And after I got a sprung gusset in the service of the state."

"Still, he's tough," Retief conceded.

"Well, yes. Hiff knows how to take a fall. And now, if you'll just follow me, Retief—"

"I'll follow you to Ambassador Shiss. Keep in mind that I have an easy-access blast pistol in my pocket."

"Shucks, Retief, you don't think I'd try to pull a swifty, do you?" Fith scurried ahead, across the vast hall. He stopped before a bank of unlighted, gray-painted elevator doors. In the adjacent wall was another, elaborately decorated in scarlet and gold.

"Let's take that one," Retief suggested.

"Perish, forbid!" Fith exclaimed. "That one's for the exclusive use of His Excellency."

"He won't mind if we go up in it, as long as we don't meet him coming down."

"True. But one never knows. On the other

hand, he never comes to the main hall from the
Chancery Tower. So I suppose we're safe."

They rode up uneventfully. Mirrors on two
walls reflected the tall, powerfully built Terran
dressed in a late mid-afternoon sub-informal coverall with the CDT crest on the pocket, and
beside him the spindle-legged Groaci in the drab
hip-cloak and dun eye-shields.

The third wall was occupied by an array of
control buttons of many colors and shapes beneath a placard reading:

PERIL! ONLY ONE CONTROL SWITCH IS
NOT BOOBY-TRAPPED. THE OFFICER OF THE
DAY HAS THE CODE. THE SAFE BUTTON
WILL OPEN THE DOORS AT THE CHANCERY
LEVEL. ALL OTHERS WILL DETONATE AN
EXPLOSIVE CHARGE.   AUTHORIZED PER-
SONNEL ONLY. SIGNED: THE AMBASSADOR.

The car stopped. A faint humming sound was
audible.

"Seen the Officer of the Day lately?" Retief
inquired.

"To have trapped you neatly, impetuous Soft
One!" Fith hissed. "To be no way out for you
now. As for myself, I expire with enthusiasm.
My only regret is that I can only experience
self-immolation once in line of duty. So to get
on with it."

"Very dramatic," Retief said, "but pretty silly.
Just get busy and open up, Fith. No one will
ever know that you skipped your big chance to
do your closing number."

"Wild Goroonian Glump-beasts could not
wring the secret from me, vile Terry!"

"Why would they try?" Retief wondered aloud.
"I'll bet a valuable collector's item against a

plain set of Taiwan-made eye-shields you'll be eating lunch in half an hour with your appetite intact."

"Never, crass violater of hallowed Groacian tradition!" Fith shifted position, folded his arms, and leaned back against the wall.

At once colored lights flashed, buzzers buzzed, beepers beeped, and a faint odor of Celestial Queen incense was wafted on the air. The elevator doors slid smoothly open.

"Drat! I blew it!" Fith said casually, moving away from the treacherous control panel.

"Sure you did. It was the thought of lunch that confused you," Retief said soothingly. "Anybody could have made the same mistake. You can go play in the sand now, Fith. If I need you I'll call."

"You're a regular guy, Retief," Fith said, in his fluent Terran. He wedged himself into a corner of the car in an attempt to disappear.

The room on which the doors opened was a spacious chamber with wide windows overlooking the Embassy fungus gardens. The walls were panelled in pale yellow blinwood, and hung with richly brocaded tapestries that Retief recognized as of Fufian manufacture.

At the far side of the room, behind a wide desk inlaid in violet-dyed tump leather, sat Ambassador Shiss. He was unusually scrawny even by Groacian standards, but richly arrayed in a pink velvet tunic of Terran cut adorned with scarlet aiguillettes, purple shoulder-boards with Major General insignia and gold Austrian knots. His platinum eye-shields were jewel-encrusted.

"What's this?" he barked in perfect Terran. "Fith, I see you skulking there in my personal

VIP lift. What's the meaning of conducting this interloper into the Presence—and unannounced at that?"

"Why, hi there, sir," Fith chirped. "I hope you don't mind our popping in. Under the circumstances one had no time to phone ahead for an appointment."

"Skip it, Private Fith. You'd better hang up your jock when you report in for confinement to quarters. Your career is at an end." The irate Ambassador turned a pair of eyes on Retief, keeping three on Fith. "Now, as for you, Retief—" he began. "Wait a minute," he interrupted himself, "where's Magnan?"

"My colleague was detained on a cultural exchange with headsman Nith," Retief said.

"Is that damn fool playing with his Roy Rogers films again? He was up here a few minutes ago, asking about a missing projector. But no matter—I didn't summon you here to blather about trivia."

"That's right, Your Excellency."

"Eh? What's right?"

"You didn't summon me here," Retief said.

"And you'll have a heck of a time leaving without an invitation. To you this gracious structure may appear no more than an ordinary masterpiece of Groacian institutional architecture, but beneath its homey exterior lies the framework of a Groaci Number Nine fortress, of the type we normally use on these crude, outpost worlds."

"Consider me deeply impressed," Retief said. "Where's Foreign Minister D'Ong?"

"Your insolence would be insupportable, if I did not feel a need to talk to a fellow-diplomat

about D'Ong. You may be seated, Retief. And as
for you, Fith," the Ambassador added, swivel-
ling an eye-stalk to the cowering figure in the
elevator, "kindly remove yourself to the sub-
dungeon."

The elevators doors slid shut.

Retief pulled out the deep easy chair beside
the desk and seated himself. He lit up a dope-
stick and puffed smoke at the Groaci, causing
the latter to snap his nostrils shut after a single
snort of irritation.

"You know I hate those stinky dope-sticks,"
Shiss said in a thin voice, "Which is doubtless
why you lit it. But I'm determined not to let you
distract me by these petty tactics."

"Let's get back to D'Ong," Retief suggested.
"And this is a top-quality Groaci Hoob-flavored
stick I'm smoking."

"Um. Let us place our fingering pieces on the
table. Naturally I recognize that Terra, like
Groac, must interest itself in Grote. Freddy gave
a lunch for D'Ong this afternoon. Did D'Ong
leave at the time prescribed by protocol?"

"He left, at any rate," Retief said. "We don't
hustle Foreign Ministers into our Embassy and
lock them away."

"Neither do the Groaci—at least," Shiss added,
with a brief thrashing of eye-stalks, "not Foreign Ministers we hope to persuade into treaty
relationships. True, we hurried D'Ong away from
Magnan's perfidious attempt to intercept him.
True, we installed D'Ong in a High Security
room—luxuriously furnished—in which he could
stay until he made his decision. But he won't
decide! He's just staying!"

"Doesn't sound like Minister D'Ong," Retief

said. "He's very sensitive to the feelings of others, and punctual to a fault."

"Strange. I fear, like all inferior life-forms, a category which includes all non-Groaci—and, between us, quite a number of the Groaci—D'Ong is not to be trusted in matters of great import."

"I can't accept that, Your Excellency, without proof," said Retief.

"Proof!" Ambassador Shiss rose, with a great jingling and creaking and rustling of his attire. "Come. I'll show you."

He led Retief across the room to a bar. To the left was a panel apparently identical to that in the elevator. Shiss pressed a button. The entire bar, with its mirrored back wall, slid aside.

Retief was looking into a softly lit room, garishly paneled in deeply carved and gilded wood, and carpeted with a high-pile rug in puce and magenta, with mauve curlicues.

D'Ong, seeming rather plain in his green satin and silver braid, sat in an overstuffed chair, his eyes fixed on a small screen on which Roy Rogers' face grimaced while the soundtrack moaned of love on the range.

"Come in, Retief," D'Ong called absently. "You here, too, Shiss? Nagging me again for a decision, I suppose."

The Ambassador's eye-stalks waved wildly at the film. "The missing projector! How did it get here? Nith must be tanked to the oculars on switz-juice!" Shiss hurried off.

Retief, careful not to break the beam from the projector, circled to stand beside D'Ong. "Mr. Minister," he said, "the cavalry has arrived. Are you ready to go?"

"Goodness, no, Retief. Sit down—and don't

brush those dope-stick ashes onto the carpet. We're just getting to the good part, where Roy mounts his wench and rides off into the wasteland."

"I think you've got Trigger and Dale confused," Retief said, sinking into a nearby chair and stubbing the dope-stick out in a Ming bowl.

"I confess I pay little attention to names, but how I admire the *savoir faire* of the cowpersons, who, in times of strife, think first of love. Always they and their faithful mates couple joyously as they dash off across the plains, hero and villain alike. Silly of me to be so sentimental, I know, but nostalgia is such sweet sadness. How it reminds me of my honeymoon with C'lunt, so long ago."

"Understandable, of course."

"One would have to know dear C'lunt to empathize fully. He's such a darling."

"*He*? Then you're female?"

"You're surprised?"

"No, not really," Retief said, after a moment of thought. "I might have guessed that your charm and sensitivity are feminine. It was stupid of me to confuse you with a male."

"It certainly *was* stupid, Retief. Our males are only seven inches in height."

"I don't think I've ever met a male Grotian socially."

"Oh, no. They don't mingle. The dear creatures tend to feel inferior, being only seven inches tall. Sometimes they feel quite low indeed. That's why, when I saw the creatures in the pudding—"

"You associated them with Grotian males, and whoofled."

"Yes. Oh, dear," she sighed, as the reel whirred

with a slapping of the film end. "That was beautiful."

Retief rose and shut down the projector. "How did you obtain the film equipment?"

"Well, Retief, frankly I was bored. Ambassador Shiss was so thoughtful, escorting me into this lovely room and securing the entry. I had almost made up my mind to sign the Terran treaty. I felt Terra and Grote had so much in common. The females wear gorgeous attire and revel at social functions, while the males are drab and do the menial labor. And then, too, Terra could provide every Grote household with a tea-bag.

"But I had to see what Groac had to offer. I waited for the Ambassador to enter and place his proposals before me. But he only nagged me and kept the entryway secured. So I got bored. I wondered what the Groaci had done with poor Mr. Magnan—so I whoofled."

"You—er—whoofled to the dungeons?"

"I *meant* to whoofle there, but I was uncertain of the Embassy floor plans. I found myself in a dank stone room where a leather-aproned Groaci was viewing these precious films. He did not see me in the darkness. After he left, I—well, it was bad protocol, I know—I twaffled the equipment and the round tins of film up here.

"I shouldn't say so, Retief, but I'd about decided to sign the Groaci treaty, if I could have the Roy Rogers love story. Selfish of me, isn't it?"

"Not at all, D'Ong," Retief smiled. "But those are Terran films. Sign with Terra, and you'll get all the Roy Rogers films. And Gene Autry and the lot. Not to mention Nelson Eddy and the

Andrews Sisters. I think I could promise you Vera Hruba Ralston."

"Oh, Retief, how sublime! The Terran treaty is as good as signed!"

"I heard that!" wheezed Ambassador Shiss's hoarse voice from the entry panel. "Never will Groac accept such humiliation! Minister D'Ong, you and Retief will stay in that room until you agree to a Groaci treaty!"

He stepped back. The entire bar slid into place again and sealed with a complex click.

Retief commented, "Now we'll be getting bored together, Madam Minister."

"Goodness, no. We can whoofle," D'Ong said casually.

"*You* can whoofle. I can't," Retief said.

"Yes, that *is* tiresome. And the Terran metabolism would probably suffer from being twaffled through a metal door. But cheer up, Retief," D'Ong said. "I shall whoofle out and twaffle you free. If you can prevail upon Ambassador Shiss to allow us to exit through his office—"

"My hand blaster will suffice for that maneuver," Retief said. "But, Madam D'Ong, the bar panel is a suicide device. One touch—"

"I can twaffle without touching, and I shall stand well back. You'd better do the same, Retief."

She abruptly vanished.

Retief prudently distanced himself from the entry wall. He drew his hand blaster. When the wall went up in smoke, he intended to have the drop on Ambassador Shiss.

"Well, Ben, a bath and a fresh coverall have improved you considerably," Ambassador Smallfrog observed, lolling back in his hip-o-matic. "Coming home in a Yill garbage truck!"

"I was thankful enough for F'Lin-lin's help in escaping the Groaci, Mr. Ambassador," Magnan said, stroking his brow. "My head is still a-whirl after my harrowing experience."

"Um. Mustn't brood, Magnan. Pity we can't send a squad of Marines over there to search the Groaci compound from ridge-pole to refuse-pits and catch the scamps red-handed with D'Ong and Retief. But, of course, to violate a friendly embassy would be unthinkable."

"Let's think about it anyway," Magnan suggested.

"Surely you're joking," Smallfrog said icily. "As convention-abiding bureaucrats, we have no choice but to chalk one up for Shiss and his boys, after which we can rest on our oars until morning, when Shiss proceeds to express regrets to the Grotian Foreign Office. A pity poor D'Ong was seized and compelled into durance vile. I suppose he naively revealed the magic tea-bag to Shiss just as carelessly as he did to us. Magnan, do you believe in magic?"

"No, of course not. But the whoofling and twaffling happened all the same."

"It would be injudicious of me, as a senior officer, to say whether those things are possible or impossible. These trivia are outside our interest cluster. I merely assigned to you the task of ferreting out the secret of the four-cup tea bag. That does not imply an interest in parlor tricks."

"But where's Retief?" Magnan queried his chief. "We can't just forget the whole matter and abandon him to his fate in a Groaci dungeon."

"I suppose you're right, Ben. In spite of the

fact that the fellow clearly exceeded instructions in going so far as to attempt something actually constructive, certain small-minded critics of the corps might adopt a negative, or even antagonistic, attitude, were it known he disappeared forever under unconventional circumstances."

"Quite. And all for naught. We still don't have the secret of the magic tea bag," Magnan mourned.

"Harrumph. We must avoid the use of the word 'magic,' Ben. Once again, you risk laying this Mission—and even myself—or *your*self—open to criticism. I think 'miraculous tea-bag' communicates the essentials without the undignified connotations of the other term."

"Gosh, yes, Your Excellency. I was just thinking how you go right to the heart of a matter, side-stepping the pitfalls that trap lesser bureaucrats."

"To be sure, Ben. Still, one can't help wondering what Shiss is doing with Retief."

The French windows swung open.

Magnan yelped and grabbed for suddenly flying papers as Retief and Foreign Minister D'Ong stepped into the room.

"Retief! And Mr. Minister!" Magnan cried. "Goodness knows you've had His Excellency and myself on tenterhooks, wondering what happened to you. And here you are, safe and sound. Heavens, you could at least give a person warning before appearing out of nowhere like that!"

"Not out of nowhere, precisely, Ben," Ambassador Smallfrog corrected gently. "They came through the windows, quite obviously. Excellency, pray take a chair. Retief, there'll be an entry in your file regarding your rather excessive zeal in invading a friendly embassy."

"I thought the signing of the Grote-Terra trade treaty was worth the bending of a few rules," Retief said.

"Why, Mr. Minister—" Smallfrog began.

"It's Madam Minister," Retief interposed.

"Madam!" The Ambassador and his First Consul exclaimed at once.

D'Ong shook her green satin robe impatiently. "Yes, Freddy, you'll find it quite natural when you get used to it. While Retief is explaining the treaty to you, dear Ben can take me to the projection room, where the film stacks might have a Hopalong Cassidy."

"Of course, Ben, escort Her Excellency immediately," Smallfrog ordered.

When the pair had left the room, Smallfrog turned to Retief. "So D'Ong is a female! I never realized! How are we to avoid such a horrible blunder in future?"

"Easily. Grotian males are seven inches tall. Really, Mr. Ambassador, we mustn't serve shrimp cocktail again."

"Retief, my head is positively spinning," the Ambassador declared. "All the regulations you've broken are passing in review in front of my eyes."

"May I interrupt the long tailback to discuss the treaty?"

"Yes, first things first. What do the Grotians want?"

"A tea-bag in every pot, and Nelson Eddy on every video. In return," Retief explained, "we are permitted to call upon the Grotians for whoofling, twaffling, and quaffling."

"I have seen the whoofling and twaffling. But what is quaffling?"

Retief took D'Ong's scarf from his pocket.

Smallfrog blurted, "Why, I saw D'Ong wrap the tea-bag in that scarf at lunch!"

"Yes," Retief said, unwrapping the inexhaustible bag. "D'Ong apparently carries it everywhere, renewing it by quaffling."

"And quaffling is—?"

"The indefinite replacement of used atoms. Quaffling is why the Grotians live for hundreds of years. And why the tea-bag is ever fresh. Of course, as D'Ong says, one can't quaffle forever. Then the only recourse is to furfle."

"And what is furfling?"

"I fear it would be counter-productive, Mr. Ambassador," Retief said seriously. "Furfling is done only by the deceased. I don't think we really want to know how to furfle."

"Oh, quite right, Retief. Quite right."

END

HERE IS AN EXCERPT FROM <u>ROGUE BOLO</u>, THE BRAND-NEW NOVEL BY KEITH LAUMER COMING FROM BAEN BOOKS IN JANUARY 1986:

Alone in darkness unrelieved I wait, and waiting I dream of days of glory long past. Long have I awaited my commander's orders, too long: from the advanced degree of depletion of my final emergency energy reserve, I compute that since my commander ordered me to low alert a very long time has passed, and all is not well.

My commander is of course well aware that I wait here, my mighty potencies leashed, my energies about to flicker out. One day when I am needed he will return, of this I can be sure. Meanwhile, I review again the multitudinous data in my memory storage files.

A chilly late-summer-morning breeze gusted along Main Street, a broad and well-rutted strip of the pinkish clay soil of the world officially registered as GPR 7203-C, but known to its inhabitants as Spivey's Find. The street ran aimlessly up a slight incline known as Jake's Mountain. Once-pretentious emporia in a hundred antique styles lined the avenue, their façades as faded now as the town's hopes of development. There was one exception: at the end of the street, crowded between weather-worn warehouses, stood a broad shed of unweathered corrugated polyon, dull blue in color, bearing the words CONCORDIAT WAR MUSEUM blazoned in foot-high glare letters across the front.

Two boys came slowly along the cracked plastron sidewalk and stopped before the sign posted on the narrow, dried-up grass strip before the high, wide building.

" 'This structure is dedicated to the brave men and women of New Orchard who gave their lives in the Struggle for Peace, AE 2031-36. A sign of progress under Spessard Warren, Governor,' " the taller of the boys read aloud. "Some progress," he added, kicking a puff of dust at the shiny sign. " 'Spessard.' That's some name, eh, Dub?" The boy spat on the sign, watched the saliva run down and drip onto the brick-dry ground.

"I'll bet it was fun, being in a war," Dub said. "Except for getting kilt, I mean."

"Come on," Mick said, starting back along the walk that ran between the museum and the adjacent warehouse. "We don't want old Kibbe seeing us and yelling," he added, *sotto voce*, over his shoulder.

In the narrow space between buildings, rank yelloweed grew tall and scratchy. The wooden warehouse siding on the boys' left was warped, the once-white paint cracked and lichen-stained.

"Come on," Mick called, and the smaller boy hurried back to his side. Mick had halted before an inconspicuous narrow door set in the plain plastron paneling which sheathed the sides and rear of the museum. NO ADMITTANCE was lettered on the door.

"Come on." He turned to the door, grasped the latch lever with both hands, and lifted, straining.

"Hurry up, dummy," he gasped. "All you got to do is push. Buck told me." The smaller boy hung back.

"What if we get caught?" he said in a barely audible voice, approaching hesitantly. Then he stepped in and put his weight against the door.

I come to awareness after a long void in my conscious existence, realizing that I have felt a human touch! Has my commander returned at last? After the last frontal assault by the Yavac units of the enemy, in the fending off of which I expended my action emergency reserves, I recall that my commander ordered me to low alert status. The rest is lost.

My ignorance is maddening. Have I fallen into the hands of the enemy . . . ?

There are faint sounds, at the edge of audibility. I analyze certain atmospheric vibratory phenomena as human voices. Not that of my commander, alas, since after two hundred standard years he cannot have survived, but has doubtless long ago expired after the curious manner of humans; but surely his replacement has been appointed. I must not overlook the possibility, nay, the likelihood that my new commandant has indeed come at last. Certainly, someone has come to me—

For
Fiction with Real Science In It, and Fantasy That Touches The Heart of The Human Soul . . .

Baen Books bring you Poul Anderson, Marion Zimmer Bradley, C.J. Cherryh, Gordon R. Dickson, David Drake, Robert L. Forward, Janet Morris, Jerry Pournelle, Fred Saberhagen, Michael Reaves, Jack Vance . . . all top names in science fiction and fantasy, plus new writers destined to reach the top of their fields. For a free catalog of all Baen Books, send three 22-cent stamps, plus your name and address, to

Baen Books
260 Fifth Avenue, Suite 3S
New York, N.Y. 10001